THE HAPPY HOSTAGE

When an agreement is made with the U.S.A. to build missile bases in Carmania, Elisabeth Renner and her friends plot to kidnap the American ambassador to Carmania and force the agreement to be cancelled. However, they get the wrong man: Charles Gresham, a budding British business tycoon. And he soon finds himself sympathising with his pretty captor. Then Elisabeth reluctantly decides to call it all off, and things really go wrong — when Charles doesn't want to be released!

CHARLES STUART

THE HAPPY HOSTAGE

Complete and Unabridged

LINFORD
Leicester

First published in Great Britain in 1975 by
Robert Hale & Company
London

First Linford Edition
published 2009
by arrangement with
Robert Hale Limited
London

British Library CIP Data

Stuart, Charles
    The happy hostage.—Large print ed.—
Linford romance library
    1. Love stories
    2. Large type books
    I. Title
    823.9′2 [F]

    ISBN 978–1–84782–565–0

Published by
F. A. Thorpe (Publishing)
Anstey, Leicestershire

Set by Words & Graphics Ltd.
Anstey, Leicestershire
Printed and bound in Great Britain by
T. J. International Ltd., Padstow, Cornwall

This book is printed on acid-free paper

for
Nancy and Gordon

1

'There is only one thing to do then,' said Elisabeth, 'It's obvious.'

'What's that?' asked Rudolf Renner, her brother.

'We must kidnap the American Ambassador and hold him to ransom. It works in other countries, so why shouldn't it work here?'

There was a hushed silence. 'Kidnap the American Ambassador?' asked Kurt Schwarz in an awed voice. He looked at Elisabeth wonderingly. Were his ears deceiving him? Could she possibly be serious?

'That's right. It shouldn't be difficult. It isn't as though he has a bodyguard or anything like that. I daresay it's quite easy to kidnap someone if they're not expecting it.'

'Liz,' her brother pleaded patiently, 'don't be silly. What would we do with

1

him? We'd have to take him somewhere and guard him and feed him. It isn't just a matter of pushing him into the back of a car and driving off.'

Elisabeth smiled at her brother. 'It can't be beyond our ingenuity. It's been done in so many places.'

'Yes, by revolutionaries and people like that. Nobody's ever been kidnapped here in Carmania.'

'We could keep him in the cottage near Rindt,' she went on, ignoring this last remark. 'It's quiet and well hidden in the mountains.'

'It's much too risky,' Willi Fischer protested.

'I wish you'd all stop arguing, unless someone has any better suggestion. The Americans will do anything to get their Ambassador back,' Elisabeth stated firmly.

'What will happen to us afterwards?' asked Rudolf. 'That's the question.'

'No one will ever find out who we were. Look here, we merely kidnap him and send a message to the Embassy, with a copy to the Prime Minister and the newspaper, saying that the defence agreement must be cancelled and then they'll get him back. They cancel the agreement, we smuggle him back into the city somehow and let him go. They won't know who did it, and they'll never risk going back on their word in case worse happens next time. It's all plain sailing.'

She sighed. 'I wish they hadn't signed that agreement yesterday. Nobody wants us to have an atomic missile base. Carmania hasn't been mixed up in a war for over five hundred years, and people want to keep it that way. Once we get the American base our neutrality is finished. It's all because of this oil. Sometimes I wish they'd never discovered it.'

'The oil has been very useful to Carmania,' her brother said placatingly.

'We should never have given the Americans a contract to develop the oil fields for us. I've nothing against the Americans. I like them. It's just that now they're here, they want to involve us in the arms race. However the Assembly voted in favour of the new agreement and it has been signed. Either we accept it, or we must do something drastic, and do it quickly. Can anyone think of anything better than my plan?'

They looked at one another. There were seven of them sitting round the table in the prim parlour of Willi Fischer's farmhouse at Seyden, near the foothills of the Cascamite Mountains, some twenty kilometres from Borgrad, the capital. There was Willi himself, twenty-three, an only child who had inherited his land from his father a year ago. There were the 'three G's' — Hans Grotben, a twenty-eight year-old teacher in Borgrad; Dirk Gerlach, a twenty-one year-old university student; and Walther Gruneberg who was twenty-three and who worked in his father's hotel business. Sitting next to Elisabeth was Kurt Schwarz, the oldest of them all. He was thirty, another schoolteacher, of medium height and slim build, with sun-bleached blond hair. He had been particularly friendly towards Elisabeth for the last two years and everyone wondered why they hadn't married.

Elisabeth and Rudolf Renner were the ringleaders, and Elisabeth herself the real driving force of the group. She was twenty-six, dark haired, with a lovely figure and an enchanting smile. She was a secretary in the Ministry of Foreign Affairs and a Ban The Bomb supporter. She certainly didn't want any atomic missile bases in little Carmania, an independent Grand Duchy of 1,153,134 acres, a little larger than Somerset and somewhat smaller than Lancashire. Her brother Rudolf, two years older, was an electronics engineer and another convinced pacifist.

Elisabeth had recently invented a name for them — the Committee for Carmanian Neutrality — but in fact they were all friends and members of the Borgrad Music Society, who had fallen under the influence of the vivacious and pretty girl who was now trying to persuade them to break the law.

'It needs thinking about,' Kurt remarked quietly. He didn't want to pour too much cold water on Elisabeth's ideas. He was much too fond of her. In any event he was a man who thought at least twice before he did anything, whether it was getting up in the morning or buying a new suit at the beginning of the year.

There was a murmur of assent.

'Besides,' said Hans Grotben, folding his arms, 'it's all very well saying that we can do this and that, but it needs careful planning. There's a *lot* to think about. It isn't a question of saying, 'yes, let's kidnap him'. When, where, how do we kidnap him? When, where, how do we hide him? When, where, how do we communicate with the Embassy; and when, where, how do we get him back without being caught ourselves? A lot of questions, my friends.'

'Oh you make it sound so complicated,' Elisabeth retorted impatiently. 'These are easy questions. I've already thought out some of the answers. A little bit of discussion, a few ideas from the rest of you, and we will have a complete blueprint.'

'Suppose they say 'no deal'?' asked Dirk, the youngest. 'What shall we do then?'

'Say no? They *can't*,' Elisabeth protested.

'What if they did?' Dirk insisted.

'We'd threaten to kill him,' Elisabeth decided briskly. 'Yes, that's what we'd do. We'd say, 'If you don't agree to our terms we'll execute him at midnight tomorrow.' That's what we'd do.'

'Why midnight?' Rudolf enquired.

'Well it sounds more sinister,' his sister explained. 'It isn't as though we are actually *going* to execute him. We shan't harm him at all, just kidnap him for a little while. Why, there's hardly anything wrong with it.'

'Police Chief Braun won't mind at

all,' Walther said sarcastically. 'If he catches us, he'll pat us on our heads and tell us not to be naughty again.' His voice changed. 'We could probably get life imprisonment for this. Maybe worse. I wonder what the penalty for kidnapping is, anyway. And a foreign diplomat too, to say nothing of threatening to murder him. I think it's madness.'

'You would,' Elisabeth snorted, displeased by his opposition. 'Perhaps you'd better keep out of this; stick to making sure the beds are properly made in your father's four hotels.'

'There's no need to be nasty, Elisabeth,' Walther protested, colouring. 'It's just that it's such a wild idea. Couldn't we have a demonstration or something?'

'The students did, two weeks ago,' Dirk pointed out thoughtfully.

'They only marched. We could lie down in the middle of Murrenstrasse and stop all the lunchtime traffic,' suggested Walther.

'The police would drag us to the kerb, that's all,' Elisabeth forecast. 'They might charge us with disturbing the peace, but nobody would cancel the agreement just because seven of us lay down in the street ... or seventy, for that matter. If we could get seven hundred to lie down in the streets for a week while other people brought them food and drink, that would be better — but it would be impossible.'

'Thank God for that,' murmured Rudolf.

'Well I didn't mean it seriously. Where would we get seven hundred people? We could pretend to be Arab guerrillas,' Elisabeth exclaimed animatedly, getting back to the main topic. 'That would scare them all to death. We could call ourselves the Black Mambas or the Green Februaries, or something.'

'I don't really think anyone would believe that the Arabs give a hoot about a missile base in Carmania,' Kurt told her. 'If they thought we were real

Carmanian revolutionaries, it might just possibly work.'

'That's more like it, Kurt. What do you all say?'

'Just how would we go about it?' Hans Grotben asked. 'You said you had some ideas, Elisabeth.'

'Yes, listen.'

She explained to them in some detail just how much she had worked out already and soon they were discussing points of procedure. It kept them busy till Willi suggested that it was time his widowed aunt, who lived on the farm with him, made them some coffee.

'What about it then?' Elisabeth demanded, sitting back. 'Are we going to do it? The only real problem is not to get ourselves caught.'

'We'll think about it,' Kurt answered.

'Oh Kurt, you're so cautious. I don't see how you can possibly teach anyone mathematics when you can't make up your mind about anything. Have you decided yet what one and one are?'

Kurt Schwarz coloured, and Willi got up.

'I'll order coffee,' he said firmly. 'Why don't we think it over, and when we meet in Borgrad on Wednesday at the Music Circle we can go afterwards to Elisabeth and Rudolf's house and make up our minds definitely, one way or the other. Yes or no. It's quite obvious that if we decide it is yes, we can work out the details all right. The seven of us can certainly do that. It's simply a question of deciding. All right?'

There they left it. After coffee they drove back to Borgrad where all of them lived, except their host, Willi Fischer. Elisabeth and Rudolf travelled together in her small red Volkswagen.

'You do get wild ideas, Liz,' he remarked idly as he enjoyed the afternoon sunshine and the view of rich farmland spread all round them. 'What made you think of kidnapping? When you told me you had a new idea, I never thought of that.'

'Because there's so much of it going

on,' she answered. 'First it was kidnapping diplomats, now it's mostly hijacking aeroplanes, but it's the same thing. However we're not like the others, Rudi. It's only a matter of keeping the missiles out of Carmania. We don't want to hurt anyone, or have dangerous people released from prison, or ask for a billion marks, or anything. Just leave our country the way it's been for centuries. I don't see anything wrong with that.'

'Perhaps not,' Rudolf agreed dryly, 'but there will be an enormous uproar if the American Ambassador is kidnapped. I can just imagine the newspapers and the television announcers. They say Ambassador McCudden is a personal friend of the President of the United States, a sort of protegé. Gosh, talk about unleashing a tiger.'

'That's just what we want to do,' his sister agreed complacently. 'Between now and Wednesday evening you and I must work on those details, for they're important. I want to have all the answers ready for when the others agree.'

'If they agree.'

'They will,' she predicted confidently.

*   *   *

Charles Gresham liked Carmania. It was his second visit in a month and he was glad to be back. This time, if all went well, he would conclude some important business within a very short space of time, and be able to enjoy a week's holiday in the Ewald Mountains before flying back to Frankfurt for some more meetings, and then on to London and New York.

He was a busy person, Charles Gresham, always on the go. His life was wrapped up in the industrial empire of which he was chairman. It had been founded by his father, who retained the controlling interest in it, but Charles regarded it very much as his personal birthright.

He was a pleasing looking man, an inch under six feet, broad of build, with a ready smile and warm grey eyes. His hair was brown and wavy, worn short at the back and sides, and he looked like the sportsman he was. Tennis in summer, ski-ing in winter, and golf all the year round kept him alert and in good physical trim.

He sat, relaxed and confident, across the big polished desk from Otto Walther, the Minister for Trade and Commerce. He conversed in fluent, idiomatic German and it was difficult sometimes to realise that he was English and hadn't known a word of German till he was fifteen.

'We've looked into the question of manpower,' Otto Walther said, puffing on his cigarette. 'There should be no difficulty in filling all but the few top technical posts, which we have discussed already. The Prime Minister was very impressed by the scale of employment.'

'Two thousand jobs,' Charles said quietly.

'Yes, two thousand jobs and a great deal of foreign exchange, which is always very useful. There will be no trouble over entry and work permits for the twenty-seven people you will be bringing in from outside.'

'Work permits without any time limit,' Charles insisted. 'I don't want to be told in three years' time that a permit can't be renewed. If I say a man is needed, it is my word that counts.'

'Naturally, Mr. Gresham.'

'That will be clearly stated in the agreement?'

'Yes it will, up to a total of fifty persons. When do you propose to start?'

'I don't see why we can't have all this signed up legally in two days, do you? The land is lying idle, so there are no complications over the agreement about the site. Within forty-eight hours of the lease being signed, I'll have a team of twenty men here. Of course they are only temporary, most of them. One year permits will do in the first instance. It should be possible to start clearing the site right away, and construction will go straight on from there. We can start the whole thing rolling as fast as we can get the paperwork done. We'll be in production next year. You've seen the phased schedule already. It's really up to you, sir.'

'Today is Friday. We can have the main agreement ready for signature on Monday afternoon at three,' Otto Walther answered. 'The lease for the land will take two days longer. That brings us to Wednesday, say about five o'clock. All signed up by then. How does that do?'

'Splendid. My first batch of people will be here on Friday afternoon, I'll brief them on Saturday, and then I'm doing something unusual.'

'What's that?' the Minister asked.

'I'm taking a week off. I've heard a great deal about Karaveran. You've got a big country club up there with a good golf course.'

'The Doppler Club. It is internationally famous.'

'I know. I want a week away from everything. I've got a heavy summer

schedule and I shan't have a that'
chance of a holiday till Christ

'We're very honoured that
spending your holiday here. I
won't be disappointed in the Doppler.
Everything is first class.'

'So I've been told. Also it is quiet.'

'At those prices quietness is assured,'
Otto laughed. 'It is for the wealthy.'

'Well then, if the Prime Minister is
satisfied with all the documents and
plans, there's no more to say till
Monday at three. I like the way you do
business here. Much quicker than in
most places.'

'We don't have a great deal of a
bureaucracy in Carmania,' the Minister
chuckled. 'It's usually easy to get
decisions from top people. I wonder if
you'd care to come to my house tonight
for dinner?'

'That's very kind of you.'

'I can send a car to your hotel at
eight. Would that be all right?'

'Yes thank you, it would. I have to go
to the American Embassy now, and

ѕ all for today.'

Do you do business with the Americans here in Carmania?'

'No, no. I'm not interested in their oil. I happen to know a friend of the American Ambassador, someone I met recently in Washington. I often visit the States. We have some factories over there.'

'Mr. McCudden is a very pleasant man. We like him here in Carmania.'

'What about this defence agreement with America? I understand a lot of people are opposed to it.'

'Naturally there are some who would stand in the way of progress, but I wouldn't say feelings run high. The question was properly debated and put to the vote in the Assembly.'

'You're becoming quite involved with the U.S.A. aren't you?'

'I suppose so. They discovered the oil and they're recovering it. We receive very handsome royalties indeed, quite apart from what the oil company spends here, which is considerable. We don't mind obliging them over their defence plans.'

'I was a little surprised,' Charles replied. 'I thought you'd stick to your strong neutral line. You've always avoided involvement like the plague.'

'Our neutrality is important to us. With a large atomic missile base here, our neutrality may be strengthened, may it not?'

'Yes, or else the threat to you may become greater. It all depends. I hope it works out to your satisfaction.'

'Do you disapprove, Mr. Gresham?'

'I don't know. Business is business, and running a country is just another form of business. I suppose you've got to consider it objectively. I've got rather a soft spot for small independent states like Carmania, Baratavia next door, Liechtenstein, Luxembourg, Monaco, Andorra and San Marino. I hate seeing them becoming involved in the international political scene.'

'Why? Do you expect us to stagnate?'

'Of course not. I suppose I'm always afraid the little countries will be swallowed up by the bigger ones, the way small businesses are disappearing. It would be a pity. Europe would lose something important — individuality.'

'You're very romantic for an international businessman.'

'Probably just reaction,' Charles laughed. 'Well, I must go. I'll see you later this evening. Thank you very much for the invitation.'

He left the big Ministry building and took a taxi to the American Embassy, a few streets away. He had already made an appointment and Jason McCudden did not keep him waiting long. He had heard of Belmont Industries International and was curious to meet its chairman.

They shook hands and Jason sent out for coffee. Charles refused a cigarette.

'You're pretty young looking to be chairing a company the size of Belmont,' Jason McCudden said pleasantly.

'You're pretty young to be an Ambassador, aren't you? If it's of any interest, I'm thirty-six. I took the trouble to find out that you're thirty-eight, a personal friend of the President, disgustingly rich, and apparently content to be stuck in a small country like Carmania, which only just rates an embassy.'

'You have been doing your homework,' the Ambassador laughed.

'Don Houston told me a lot about you, so I'm cheating,' Charles laughed. 'I'm involved in some business with his group of companies and when he heard I was coming to Borgrad he said to be sure to look you up. And here I am,' he added, making a gesture with his hands.

'Always glad to meet a friend of Don's. Here's the coffee.'

They drank coffee and chatted. They were very similar in size and general appearance, and one might have been excused for thinking that they were related. They had a common interest in golf, and when he heard that Charles was hoping to play at Karaveran all the following week, Jason McCudden insisted that they have a few rounds together.

'I can get away from my desk pretty

well any time I want,' he confessed. 'This is a nice quiet spot. It's about an hour's drive to the club, along a very fine mountain road. Yes, I'll gladly come and give you a few games.'

'It beats me why you stay in a place like this,' Charles said frankly. 'I like it, of course, but I couldn't spend any length of time here. It's too quiet and parochial. It's a good place to visit.'

McCudden laughed at this. 'That's what I like about it. I almost had a breakdown a couple of years back, due to strain, and the doctors recommended a long holiday. I couldn't face a long holiday so I asked the President if he couldn't fix me up with an appointment abroad that would give me an interest in life without involving me in too much stress and strain. He suggested this. It was just what I needed. I have another year to do, and then my wife and I will be returning to God's own country.'

'I see. Well, if you've got to take it easy, this must be a pleasant place to do it.'

'How about a game of golf tomorrow?' Jason suggested.

'I could manage that. I have almost a free day on my hands.'

'Come round here about eleven-thirty and I'll drive you up to the mountains for lunch. We can play in the afternoon and return to the city in the evening when we feel like it.'

'That sounds marvellous. I can do all I have to do by eleven-thirty.'

'Fine. Now let me call my car to the door to take you to your hotel.'

'That won't be necessary.'

'I insist. The car sits around all day, doing nothing much to justify its expense. Dixon, my driver, will be glad of something to do.'

He spoke into his intercom and then got up and came round to the front of the desk.

'He'll be here in a moment. I'm glad you dropped in. You see there's one big snag here. You soon get to know everybody. It's nice to meet someone new, especially someone new and interesting who happens to be a plus two handicap man. That doesn't happen often.'

Charles grinned as the intercom squawked. The car was waiting. He shook hands with the Ambassador and walked along the hall to the front door. When he reached the big stone steps he saw the Lincoln Continental in front of him. Nice car, he thought. The uniformed driver stepped forward. 'Mr. Gresham?'

'That's right. I'd like to go to the New Imperial Hotel please.'

'Very good sir.'

The door was held open and Charles stepped towards it. As he did so a small grey Volkswagen, streaked with mud and rust, drew up alongside at a slight angle, blocking the Lincoln. Two masked men got out and opened the car door, facing Charles as he bent to get into the Lincoln. Charles's eyes popped as he looked directly at two blue-black guns.

'Out,' a voice said curtly. 'Quickly. If you don't the driver will get shot as well.'

One of the two men was pointing his gun at the astonished driver. That decided Charles. He got out and allowed himself to be hustled into the V.W. In an instant it roared off, tyres squealing, even as Dixon shouted the alarm. Two passers-by had seen what had happened, but it had all been so smooth and quick that they were still standing gawping.

The Volkswagen now indulged in a series of turns into side streets until Charles lost his sense of direction. In a quiet part of town it screeched to a halt beside a bright red Volkswagen with a girl at the wheel.

At gunpoint Charles was transferred to the other car. He did think momentarily of making a dash for it, but two things prevented him. It was possible that they might shoot, which would make a break rather dangerous, and he was in a quiet cul-de-sac, which apparently led nowhere. It wasn't a good place for an escape attempt — there was nobody in sight.

So he sighed, shrugged, and sat down in the back of the red car. The two men got in beside him and the car did a U-turn and drove off, leaving the original car parked by the kerb.

'Well, well,' Charles said, stretching his legs as best he could in the confined space, 'will someone please tell me what all this is about?'

Deliberately he spoke in English. There was no reply.

'The British Ambassador won't be amused,' he pointed out mildly.

The car had arrived at a dual carriageway and now it gathered speed. Nobody spoke, so Charles folded his arms and settled back to wait.

2

The little red V.W. followed the main highway of Carmania which ran from Hoss, on the northern frontier, through Borgrad the capital, and then swept eastwards following the foothills of the Cascamites in a grand curve through Baltz, Seyden and Ender and so on to Sellberg, the industrial town on the southern frontier, bordering Austria. At Baltz, a small quiet agricultural centre, they followed a back street out of town and picked up a narrow winding road which took them into the mountains. It was a single-lane track with passing places every quarter of a mile or so. Although their destination, over two thousand metres up in the mountains, was only eight kilometres from Baltz, the distance by road was nearer fifteen.

Once they left Baltz they passed no other cars and saw no one till they arrived at the village of Rindt. This was a small ski-ing centre in winter, rarely visited by tourists, and its year-round prosperity depended on a number of chalets on the wooded slopes of the small mountain valley in which it stood, and which were week-end and holiday homes for wealthier Carmanians.

Elisabeth followed a narrow road running south past a number of chalets and finally turned into a rough track. About a mile along the track, in a clearing hidden from sight by dense bushes and tall trees, was the cottage. There were no other houses in the near vicinity. The car drew up by the long, low building and Elisabeth switched off the engine.

'A hideaway in the forest. Very convenient,' Charles said pleasantly. 'Is no one going to talk to me?'

'Please go inside.' Elisabeth said in English.

'Very well.' He went in and looked around the living room which lay behind the front door. It wasn't bad, with pine panelled walls, some nice pieces of furniture and some surprisingly gay cushions and curtains. He saw a radio standing on a shelf among some books and magazines, and a record player on a table in the corner.

Rudolf took Charles gently by the arm and showed him into one of the rooms leading off the living room. It was a small bedroom and a bed was made up in one corner.

'You will sleep here. We have provided some pyjamas and shaving things. We hope you won't have to stay very long.'

'I hope so too. Will someone please tell me what this is about?'

'Would you care to have a drink?'

'Coffee if possible. Otherwise don't bother.'

'Very well. I'll ask my sister. She will stay here and cook for you. There will be two others on guard all the time. Don't do anything silly, Mr. McCudden. We don't want to hurt you.'

Charles paused momentarily on his

way to the door. McCudden? Did they think he was Jason McCudden? If so they were in for a rude surprise. What on earth did they want from the American Ambassador, he wondered? He said nothing as he walked back into the next room. The girl was pretty, very pretty indeed, and young. What was she doing, mixed up in a stupid affair like this? The man with him had already said he was her brother, and he seemed a decent enough person. The other two were younger, much younger. One looked scarcely older than a schoolboy. They wore good clothes, their hands weren't the hands of manual workers, their shoes — always a dead give-away — were clean and smart. This was no gang of toughs. Who were they? Students? If so, who were the man and the girl who were too old to be students?

'Mr McCudden would like some coffee,' Rudolf told Elisabeth.

'Very well. For all of you?'

They nodded and she went into a

small kitchen at the back. Charles sat down, crossed his legs nonchalantly, and beamed at his captors.

'I hope you're not looking for a ransom,' he said mildly. 'I'm not sure that anyone would pay one for me.'

'You're a hostage, that's all,' Rudolf answered. 'Once the defence agreement is torn up, you'll be released.'

'So that's it? The defence agreement?' He began to see light.

'Yes,' Elisabeth said from the doorway and he glanced up at her with interest. 'That's it. We don't like it. The Assembly have voted in favour of it, so the only way we can have the agreement cancelled is by bargaining with your life.'

'Ah yes, my life. You'll kill me if they don't agree, will you?'

'Certainly,' Elisabeth lied cheerfully. 'Bit by bit, of course. First we send your ears to the Embassy, then arms and legs and things.'

'Um.' Charles made a face. 'Messy. Let's hope they tear up the agreement.

31

I mean, it will be a bit awkward if they hold out till I've got no ears, one leg and one arm, and then change their minds. It will ruin my golf handicap.'

'You don't seem worried,' Elisabeth said accusingly. He should be worried. He'd seen the dummy guns, surely? They were very good, models of the real thing, made in England. Of course they couldn't fire ammunition but it was impossible to tell that, just by looking. Walther Gruneberg had bought them, intending to use them for decoration in one of his father's hotel bars, along with a lot of other ferocious bric-à-brac.

'No point in worrying, is there?' Charles asked brightly. 'I mean, here I am, and that's all there is to it. My main worry is a cup of coffee.'

Elisabeth went back into the kitchen, made the coffee and brought in a tray of steaming mugs which she handed round. It was jolly good coffee, Charles thought, as good as he had ever tasted. If the food were as good, he ought to enjoy his very brief stay with them. He would be back in his hotel in time for dinner, of course.

'You don't look very bloodthirsty,' he said conversationally. 'What are you? Students? Communists? Maoists? No beards at all — most unprofessional.'

'We're just people,' Rudolf replied shortly. 'People who want to see Carmania stay free and neutral. We don't want American armaments in our country.'

'It seems that other people do,' Charles pointed out. 'After all, the agreement was debated in the Assembly, wasn't it, and voted on by your democratically elected representatives?'

'That's exactly where democracy falls down,' Elisabeth answered, sitting down facing him. 'We elect people to represent us, but when it comes to an issue like this there are only fifty-seven men voting, not a hundred thousand, which is the number on the electoral list. I believe that most of the Representatives voted in a way that the majority of their electors *didn't* want. The whole theory of democracy is ridiculous. The representation is only partial. Unless you had a referendum on every item before the Assembly, you couldn't possibly say that the country wanted this instead of that. You can only say that the fifty-seven want it.'

'The Heinz syndrome?' Charles suggested humorously.

'Heinz?' Elisabeth asked blankly.

'The 57 Varieties. It was a joke. So what is the answer, if you can't be satisfied with your properly elected representatives?'

'Do away with the Assembly and let the Grand Duke run things himself,' Elisabeth told him. Charles saw the three men shift uneasily, and smiled.

'A royalist. How interesting and unusual. Of course, if your Grand Duke Philip was in favour of the defence agreement, that would leave you right back where you started — only without representation in the Assembly.'

'He certainly isn't in favour of the

agreement,' she countered flatly.

'You know him?'

'No . . . but I'm sure he isn't.'

'What does it matter?' Rudolf interrupted impatiently. 'Those fools in the Assembly want a missile base here. We don't and neither do a lot of other people. So they must cancel the agreement and we will send you back alive. It's all very simple, Mr. McCudden.'

'Do you think they'll agree?' Charles asked, intrigued.

'Of course they'll agree,' Elisabeth said confidently. It was her plan, after all.

'Suppose they are crafty and only agree until I'm safe, and then go ahead with the missile bases?'

'Bases? Only one,' Elisabeth said sharply.

'Three in fact,' Charles answered blandly. 'I happen to know.'

'My God that's worse,' Elisabeth exclaimed. 'Anyway, if they did something so dishonourable we could always start sending letters through the post — the kind that explode when you open them. They'll have to give in.'

'The rule of terrorism. I don't think it will work.'

'It's only on this one agreement,' Rudolf pointed out quickly. 'We don't want any rule of terrorism.'

'You haven't thought about this much, have you?' Charles asked, and Elisabeth flushed, a fact which interested him. 'Put yourself in the Government's position. Once they cave in and obey terrorists, they'll never be safe again. Next time someone doesn't agree with them there will be another terrorist threat, perhaps against children or old people. There is only one way to deal with terrorism — fight it out to the bitter end.'

'You mean they'd let you die?' Elisabeth asked, aghast at this idea.

'More likely they'll comb the country till they find me.'

'They won't find you,' she said with more confidence. 'Not even if they come here, which they won't. There's a cellar, you see.'

'Other people will know about the cellar.'

'I don't think so. My father used to live here . . . '

'You fool,' Rudolf hissed. 'You've given the game away. Now they can trace us.'

Elisabeth looked blank. All their careful plans about never mentioning names had gone up in smoke. Mr. McCudden could tell the authorities that her father had lived in the cottage and it wouldn't be long before they come up with the name of Franz Renner, Forest Supervisor, now dead, and his two children — both very much alive.

'We'll have to swear him to secrecy,' Elizabeth countered.

'I see you trust me, which is flattering,' Charles smiled.

'On the Bible,' she said. 'You'll swear on the Bible.'

'As a matter of fact,' Charles

answered, 'I don't think I'd be inclined to say anything about you, but you really are very amateur. You should have blindfolded me when you brought me here. I could lead the police to this place.'

All four looked blankly at one another. There was more to terrorism than they had thought. Their careful planning had not been careful enough. Jason McCudden had been in their power for less than an hour and a half and already they had blundered over the blindfold and Elisabeth had given him a clue to her name and Rudolf's.

'Perhaps we shall have to kill him after all,' Dirk Gerlach said gloomily, in German.

'Don't be silly,' Elisabeth snapped.

'You could always kill me and kidnap someone else,' Charles suggested, speaking in German for the first time.

'Your German is very good,' Elisabeth complimented him.

'It ought to be. Why don't we listen to the news broadcast? I'm sure it will be interesting.'

Rudolf glanced at his watch. 'There is a news bulletin due soon. Switch on.'

Young Dirk, to whom the command was addressed, turned on the transistor. There was some music. Charles smiled at Elisabeth and raised his coffee cup in a toast and she wondered at his coolness. He looked so young and so handsome, not at all like an Ambassador. She'd seen his photographs of course, but she hadn't realised just how youthful he'd be . . . or how cool! One would imagine that he was perfectly accustomed to being kidnapped.

How she had messed things up. It was too bad. Her ascendancy over Rudolf and the others had taken a big knock today. It hadn't mattered about his seeing their faces. That had been a calculated risk. The chances of his seeing them again and recognising them were remote. Not one of them had ever met an Ambassador or was likely to. Besides, once released, he would probably be recalled to America. Not blindfolding him on the journey, however, that was an awful omission. There were new problems now. She and Rudolf might even have to leave the country. Using what for money, she mused wryly?

Then the programme changed. The music stopped and the announcer began the news bulletin rather excitedly, for 'hard' news was a rarity in Carmania.

'Mr. Charles Gresham, Chairman of the giant international organisation Belmont Industries, who has been on an official visit to Carmania, was kidnapped on the steps of the American Embassy this afternoon. It is believed that he may have been mistaken for the American Ambassador, Mr. Jason McCudden, whom he had been visiting. The two men are of similar appearance.

'Mr. Gresham, who is thirty-six, is the son of the founder of Belmont Industries. Although born in England, he has spent much of his adult life in Germany where the company has considerable interests. It is understood that he has been negotiating for the building of a factory in this country which would provide employment for up to two thousand people.

'The Prime Minister in a short statement has said that no effort will be spared to trace and rescue Mr. Gresham, and to punish his abductors. It is not yet known why the kidnapping has taken place, but the police confidently expect that some sort of demand will be made very soon. If, of course, Mr. Gresham was kidnapped instead of Mr. McCudden, he may be released voluntarily. Strict security precautions have been set up at the American Embassy, and protection has been given to Embassy staff, particularly the Ambassador.'

There was a silence as the set was switched off by Rudolf and they all stared at Charles who winked broadly.

★ ★ ★

'I tell you we must let him go,' It was Walther Gruneberg speaking. He and

41

Rudolf and Elisabeth were talking together in the spare bedroom, leaving young Dirk to guard their prisoner.

'We *can't*,' Elisabeth repeated. 'He knows too much. We must try to get him on our side before we let him go.'

'You're an optimist,' Rudolf grumbled. 'A fine mess you've made.'

'Well at least I've done something,' she flashed. 'Not just sat about, grumbling against the Government. Anyway, what I said was true. We must go ahead with this man instead of the Ambassador. He's important, after all. They won't want him killed, so we trade Mr. Gresham for the agreement.'

'Bah, if the Americans agree,' Walther scoffed. 'I wish I'd never listened to you two.'

'Coward,' Elisabeth taunted him contemptuously. 'At the first sign of trouble you want to run away. Now listen to me, both of you. Rudolf will go back to Borgrad and write a demand note, using Charles Gresham instead of Jason McCudden. Little Adolf Klein will deliver the note and the copies tonight. Walther, you and Dirk will be relieved by Rudolf later this evening. I want you both to stay in Borgrad, and I don't want Willi, Kurt or Hans to come here either. Mr. Gresham has never seen them, and he'll soon forget you. This way, just Rudolf and I take the risks.'

'Thank *you*,' Rudolf grunted.

'Poor little man,' his sister scoffed with total lack of sympathy.

'Just two of you?' Walther asked. 'Is it safe?'

'If he thinks we're armed, yes.'

'What about nights? The idea was that somebody would stay awake all night.'

'Rudi and I will take it in turns. I'll do day duty and he'll do night duty. It's only for a few days.'

'We hope,' Rudolf interposed sotto voce.

'Be quiet,' she admonished him.

'What do the rest of us do?' Walther asked. 'We're leaving all the work to you two.'

'You and Dirk have helped enormously already. You will all simply be on standby. We'll need you later to get Mr. Gresham back to Borgrad safely, without being caught.'

'I don't like it,' Walther insisted. 'If we let him go now, he may treat it as a joke and we'll be safe. If we keep him, he's bound to go to the police and then, whatever happens, you and Rudi are in the soup.'

'I'll see if I can't talk him out of giving us away. After all, I'm a girl,' she concluded triumphantly.

'Do you think he'll care about that?' Rudolf scoffed. 'He must be a millionaire. Millionaires are tough ruthless people. They don't care about anyone, not even their own wives and children. What do you think he'll care about some silly secretary in a foreign country?'

'He looks nice,' Elisabeth insisted. 'Now, you've only got a week off work, Rudi, so we must get all this over in a week. You go and write the note, arrange for its delivery and come back here with a suitcase and some things. You'll find a suitcase of mine packed all ready under my bed. Bring that too. Better bring more books.'

'What a delightful prospect,' Rudolf said sourly, thinking of his girl friend. 'Cooped up here for days. What am I to tell Emma?'

'Tell her you're going to Sellberg or somewhere on business for a few days,' Elisabeth suggested. 'You'd better go now.'

They talked for a little longer, but the truth was that nobody had anything better to suggest, except Walther's plan that they release Charles Gresham at once and treat it all as a joke. It was tempting, but Elisabeth insisted that that way the defence agreement would stand. They still had a chance, however slender, of having the agreement cancelled. They had to take it.

When they had grudgingly accepted her reasoning, Rudi left and Elisabeth went into the kitchen to make a meal.

There had been thorough preparations and the hut was well provided with creature comforts, which included a handsomely stocked larder and refrigerator. That they had got everything up to the hut without making themselves conspicuous bore testimony to their careful planning. Three of the others had each made a single car journey, during the day, when they would not be conspicuous, and brought a load to the hut.

As she busied herself over the cooker in what had been her childhood home, Elisabeth prayed that the whole scheme wasn't going to backfire on them. It was so tempting to call it off, as the men had suggested, yet there was a determined streak in her. She was not one to run away at the first hint of trouble. If the worst came to the worst, they had a cousin in Austria and they could always go there and replan their lives, she and Rudolf. The others would have nothing to fear. At least she hoped not.

'You're cook as well as colonel, are

you?' The voice interrupted her thoughts and she turned to face her prisoner.

'I beg your pardon? Colonel did you say?'

'A manner of speaking. You're the leader of the gang and also the cook.'

'Am I the leader?'

She turned back to her work.

'I think so. I got that impression. What's to eat?'

'Just a simple meal. Pork chops and vegetables. Would you like some soup?'

'No, I don't think so. I'm not particularly hungry. As a matter of fact I was supposed to dine tonight with Otto Walther, the Minister for Trade and Commerce. Tomorrow I was supposed to be playing golf with the real Jason McCudden. When were you thinking of letting me go?'

'When the agreement is torn up,' she answered calmly.

'You're going ahead with your little scheme are you? That's interesting. You think the Prime Minister will tear up the agreement rather than risk the life of a British businessman?'

'Yes. Wouldn't you?'

'I don't know. I'm not a politician.'

'You're a millionaire, aren't you?'

'Unfortunately, no. Some people might call me rich, but I'm a long way from being a millionaire. What has that to do with it, anyway?'

'All millionaires are completely ruthless, aren't they?'

'I don't really know. My father is supposed to be a millionaire but he's a born romantic. He didn't set out to become big and powerful. He just had an idea which would make a good living, and it sort of grew, and grew. Anyway, all this is beside the point. There's a defence agreement at stake, and don't forget that the Americans are important in Carmania. Think of all that lovely oil.'

'We don't need the Americans!'

'Perhaps not, but I think you did a good deal with them over the oil, and they have been helpful in other ways. Somehow I get the impression that the

Prime Minister won't want to risk upsetting the American government.'

'Oh nonsense. When it comes to it, they'll do anything to get you back.'

'I wish I had your confidence.'

'You don't sound afraid.'

'I'm not afraid,' he laughed. 'I trust myself to you implicitly. Anyone who makes coffee like that, and who can cook — I expect you can sew and knit too — must be on the side of the angels.'

'On the side of the angels,' she said quietly. 'What a strange thing to say.'

'Think about it, and you'll see why I'm not scared.'

'Even although we're armed?'

'You haven't shot anyone yet. What's your name?'

She hesitated. 'Elisabeth Renner.'

'That tall chap is your brother, isn't he?'

'Yes, Rudi. You won't learn the names of any of the others. We have to protect them.'

'Does that mean that you and your

brother are going to be the sacrificial offering? Or were you hoping to get away with it?'

'There's no harm in hoping. It all depends on you.'

'You'll have to silence me. Put me in a sack with stones and drop me in the little lake at Rindt.'

'You know the name of the village?'

'Oh yes, I've studied my map of Carmania. Well, what about it? Won't you have to bump me off?'

'We're not gangsters,' she flashed.

'No? I hope the Prime Minister never finds that out, otherwise he certainly *won't* do business with you. You must keep up the bloodthirsty appearances, you know. I should make the most spine-chilling threats if I were you. If you could get hold of a few bombs and let them off in places where they'd do no harm, it would be a useful stage effect. What are you calling yourselves? The Black Hand Gang?'

'We haven't got a name. Well . . . '

'Yes?' he prompted.

'Sometimes we call ourselves the Committee for Carmanian Neutrality.'

'That sounds too respectable. It's not revolutionary enough. I can see you need advice. I know — the Black Death.'

'The Black Death?' she asked in amazement.

'Sinister, isn't it? And beautifully blood curdling. You could call yourself the Chief Executioner. 'Tear up the agreement or we will dismember Charles Gresham and post the pieces to you, signed Chief Executioner, the Black Death.' You should type it on pink paper. It has a revolutionary flavour.'

'You seem to think it's all a joke.'

'Isn't it? I say, those chops are ready. Shall I give you a hand with the mashed potatoes?'

Elisabeth simply stared at him.

3

The driver, Dixon, had given the alarm promptly enough but by the time the police arrived on the scene there was no trace of the inconspicuous rather dirty and drab Volkswagen. The city was full of similar cars and Dixon had not taken a note of the number. Certainly no one had paid any attention to another car, a gleaming red, driven at a spanking pace by a pretty girl. Why should they? The owner of the kidnap car never even knew that it had been 'borrowed'. He had gone off with a friend for three days, in the friend's car — as Hans Grotben happened to know — and when he returned his car was parked in the road where it always was.

By seven o'clock in the evening it was obvious to several people — the Chief of Police, the Prime Minister, the Commander-in-Chief of the small army who was assisting the police, and a few others — that all enquiries were fruitless. Charles Gresham had disappeared without trace. The only thing to do was to sit back and wait.

A photograph of Charles, a blow-up of his passport photograph which they got from his hotel, was to appear in the morning's newspaper and would be shown on television that night. A description would be widely circulated and a reward of ten thousand marks would be announced for information leading to the Englishman's rescue. All frontier posts had been alerted, and there were plain clothes men at the airport and railway station. In fact, if the kidnappers had driven straight to the border, the nearest point of which was only twelve kilometres from Borgrad owing to the configuration of the country, they could have slipped across quite easily already. There were some permanent border patrols, but for the most part the border was unguarded. Carmania did not boast an iron curtain.

Even so, the Police Chief was fairly certain that Gresham was still in the country and that they would hear from the kidnappers. At seven-thirty a small boy disposed of three letters. He put one through the door of the American Embassy, another through the door of the Prime Minister's house, and the third went into the letter box of the *Borgrad News*. Nobody paid any attention to him.

The one in the Embassy was the first to be discovered, some five minutes later. It was taken upstairs to Jason McCudden who was working rather later than usual owing to the fact that the kidnapping might have been meant for him. He slit open the envelope and read the contents.

To Whom It May Concern,

Charles Gresham has been kidnapped and is being detained by Carmanian patriots. Unless a joint announcement is made within three days to the effect that the defence agreement between Carmania and the United States is cancelled and that there will be no American, or indeed any other atomic missile bases in Carmania, Mr. Gresham will be killed.

Should it be necessary to kill Mr. Gresham, we shall not hesitate to do so, but we shall then strike again in some other direction and continue to wage war on the Government until the agreement is finally terminated.

An announcement on the radio is all the notification we require. Should the Government be foolish enough to accede to our requests and then enter into a new agreement or revive the old one, we shall not be so reasonable next time.

No atomic weapons for Carmania! We are not anti-American.

'Patriot'.

I'm damned, thought Jason McCudden as he read the letter and reached for the telephone. It's that defence agreement after all. An hour later he, the Prime Minister, Dr. Bruno Jung, the Chief of Police, Heinrich Braun, and General Karl Schmidt, the Army Commander, all sat together in the Prime Minister's study in his town house.

'I think we are agreed then,' Bruno Jung said, looking at them in turn. 'We do nothing for the next two days. Nothing at all. During this time Mr. McCudden will find out from the State Department what their reaction is, and will keep in touch with me. We must be prepared for any eventuality.'

'It seems to me, Mr. Prime Minister,' Jason drawled, 'that you should be able to trace the kidnappers within twenty-four hours. The whole country is only eighteen hundred square miles, after all.'

'We have two mountain ranges, and west of Sellberg there is a large area of dense forest. Nevertheless I agree with you, Braun!'

'With General Schmidt's help I am

'sure we can trace this gang.'

'You think it's a gang, do you?' McCudden asked. 'Excuse my interest, but I was almost certainly the original target, and they may get round to me yet. Don't your intelligence or secret police boys have any suspects?'

'Of course we have suspects, and we are checking them,' Braun countered stiffly. He was very much on his dignity this evening. He regarded the kidnapping as a deliberate affront to him personally, and had not once given any real thought to the unfortunate victim.

'Had you no hint at all that there might be trouble?'McCudden pressed.

'We just don't have trouble in Carmania,' Dr. Jung said gently.

'That's true, Mr. Prime Minister. I guess you don't get much practice, do you?'

'It must be students,' General Schmidt stated categorically. He was rather a picturesque figure in the ornate uniform he wore on all occasions (in bed too, it was rumoured).

'We have not overlooked the students,' Braun snapped. 'My men are busy now looking into that aspect of the affair. Frankly I do not expect any success. It's too obvious an answer.'

'The best place to hide a letter is in the letter rack, after it has been searched once,' Jason drawled. 'Courtesy of Edgar Allan Poe. In other words, don't underrate the students even if they are obvious. Have you heard yet from Mr. Gresham's father, Mr. Prime Minister?'

'Not yet.'

'You will, and he's quite a character by all accounts. I imagine he will be here tomorrow, breathing fire and fury.'

'Oh dear,' Bruno Jung sighed. 'I know very little about Mr. Gresham except that he is Chairman of Belmont Industries with whom we are negotiating a matter of business.'

'The nickel alloys factory,' Jason murmured.

'Quite.' Jung gave him a startled look. 'Is the father still connected with the company?'

'Its major shareholder,' Jason McCudden replied. 'Charles is the Chairman, but Nigel controls the business and will do till he dies — which probably will be a very long time from now. I thought I ought to warn you about him. He's a very rich and powerful man, and although I know nothing about him other than what is published, I would guess that he is going to be in a towering rage. Mr. Charles Gresham is the only child and apple of his father's eye.'

'You appear to know a lot about him,' Braun answered suspiciously.

'My dear Chief, when my spies told me that Belmont planned to open a large factory here for the manufacture of nickel alloys, I looked up Belmont and the Gresham family. It didn't take long. Matter of fact there was a big article on Nigel Gresham and his son in *Life* which my Commercial Secretary let me see.'

'All this is rather beside the point,' Jung murmured. 'Mr. McCudden, I hope you are satisfied with the measure of protection we are providing for you and your staff.'

'I am indeed, very satisfied. I don't think there is any danger at this point. It will only arise if and when they have to stop bargaining with Gresham. Incidentally, Chief Braun, do you believe that that note really is from Carmanian patriots? Couldn't it be from some subversive foreign group who want to keep the American military presence out of Carmania?'

'It's possible. At this stage anything is possible. However they did add that rather strange closing phrase, 'We are not anti-American'. It smacks more of a local protest.'

'That's true. There is no real point in talking, is there?'Jason asked, 'Not until we have some more hard fact to discuss. I'll keep in touch, Mr. Prime Minister, and I'll also be in close touch with Washington. We will be able to work out something, I'm sure.'

'I can take it that you *do* want the agreement to stand?'the general asked.

'We do, General. I think you do too.'

'I do, personally.'

'Carmania is the ideal place from our point of view, and there will be considerable financial advantages to Carmania.'

'We know them already,' Jung said with a shrug. 'Mr. McCudden, please exercise care until this unfortunate business is over. Try not to expose yourself to risk.'

'I'll give up golf for the duration, I promise. Funnily enough, I was due to play golf with Gresham tomorrow.'

A few minutes later Jason McCudden left, followed shortly afterwards by General Schmidt. Dr. Jung offered the Chief of Police a drink, and Braun accepted.

'We can't give in to them, you know,' Braun said after sipping at his brandy.

'I know, Braun, I know.'

'Despite popular fiction, it is quite easy to conceal someone. If we are dealing with known criminals, we can be very efficient, but when it comes to

61

amateurs, when it literally could be anyone, we don't know where to start looking. You realise that it will take me many days to comb the whole country, even with army assistance?'

'Yes, Braun.'

'In the end we may find nothing.'

'I am aware of that.'

'Why don't we just broadcast the message and get Gresham back? Then we can go ahead with our defence agreement, and to hell with them. They won't find it so easy next time.'

'That is probably what we shall do,' Jung laughed. 'I'm glad you agree with me. I made up my mind as soon as I read the note — unless, of course, you can effect a rescue before the deadline.'

The two men, who had been at school together, looked at each other and smiled. Braun raised his glass and drank again. 'Some day we will catch these people, unless they just give up completely. They are almost bound to try something else at another time, and then we will be waiting. I would like to think that when the time comes, they will be dealt with very severely. We don't want terrorism in Carmania. Once ordinary decency goes by the board, no man is protected. There is no such thing as total security. We have to punish savagely and so deter other people.'

'I'm afraid you are right,' Bruno Jung sighed. 'To think that we are come to this in Carmania. The only justification for the small countries, such as ourselves, is that unlike our large and powerful neighbours, by whom we are surrounded, we are peaceful, law abiding, undemanding, unwarlike — model citizens if you like. I wonder if this defence agreement is really such a good thing? It involves us now in power politics, and we've never been involved before. I wonder if our kidnappers realise that they have made me re-examine the whole matter. Of course it is too late to go back on the agreement now, but I'm no longer so sure of my attitude as I was in the beginning.' He snorted. 'I'd give a lot to know who these terrorists of ours, are, Braun.'

'So would I,' the police chief said convincingly. 'So would I. I have a feeling that nothing is going to be quite the same in Carmania after this. Terrorists indeed! Kidnappers!' He finished his brandy at a gulp.

★   ★   ★

By a happy stroke of good fortune, Rudolf exceeded his brief. Not only did he compose the letter which was delivered unobtrusively to Jason McCudden, Bruno Jung and the editor of the daily newspaper, but he also wrote a 'Letter to the Editor'. It was good strong meaty stuff and it was published next morning along with a much padded account of the kidnapping, an interview with Jason McCudden, and the photograph of Charles.

Rudolf drove into Baltz and bought a copy of the paper. The previous evening cars had been switched again, with the help of Willi Fischer, and Rudi was now driving a black Audi. Elisabeth's red V.W. was parked in the railway station car park where it would stay till it was reclaimed.

Rudolf scanned the newspaper and then drove back to the cottage triumphantly.

'Look at that,' he said to Elisabeth, handing her the paper. 'It's all over the front page. *And* there's a letter from me to the editor inside.'

'A letter from you?'

She thumbed through until she found it. Charles, who had finished a breakfast of scrambled eggs and bacon, with warm rolls, fresh butter and marmalade, and who was starting on his third cup of coffee, came up behind and peered over her shoulder.

'Who said you could do this?' Elisabeth asked while reading.

'It was just an idea I had. What do you think of it?'

'You're in the wrong business,' Charles remarked. 'You should be a politician. Look at all this about Carmania's honour, the dignity of neutrality — I like that one, I must remember it — and some pretty hot stuff on the failure of the Representatives to vote in accordance with the desires of the people who elected them. What are you, anyway? Just as a matter of interest.'

'Electronics engineer.'

'Really? I'd never have guessed. You're with Tagrad Electronics, are you?'

'Yes.'

'Well it's not a bad letter. What do you say, Elisabeth?'

'It does no harm,' she conceded and turned to read the news on the front page. 'Oh look, they've got your photograph.'

'You've nothing to fear there,' Charles laughed, looking at it. 'Nobody could possibly recognise me. Taking passport photographs is a specialised art. I know I'm not beautiful, but I don't honestly think I look like that.'

'It's a bad photograph,' Elizabeth agreed. 'Rudi, have your breakfast and go to bed.'

Rudi, who had been up all night, nodded.

'All right. Wake me at teatime if I'm not up by then.'

'There's no hurry,' Elisabeth assured him. 'Why not have a proper rest?'

'Six hours is plenty.'

He went into the kitchen, had a bowl of cereal and some toast, drank a cup of coffee, and went off to bed. Elisabeth washed up and Charles insisted on drying.

'What do we do with ourselves today?' he asked. 'Any plans?'

'No. What do you mean?'

'It's much too fine a day to stay indoors. Can't we go for a walk?'

'And have you run away?' she asked sarcastically.

'Do you think I'd risk a bullet in the back?'

Elisabeth, who had forgotten the replica guns, swallowed.

'We . . . er . . . don't want to shoot you yet.'

'Thank you for that saving 'yet'. I feel better.' Charles laughed. 'Seriously, is there nowhere we could go?'

'There are one or two tracks through the woods.'

'You know this place quite well, don't you?'

'Yes, I was brought up in this house. My father was what they call a Forest Supervisor. He died when I was twelve and Rudi fourteen. My mother moved to Borgrad then, to a small house there. She got a pension, you see.'

'You went to school in Borgrad?'

'First we went to school in Baltz, and then school and university in Borgrad.'

'So you went to university?'

'Oh yes. I took a history degree.'

'What exactly do you do now?'

'I'm a secretary in the Ministry of Foreign Affairs.'

'Secretary? With a degree?'

She nodded and smiled. 'Why not?

I'm secretary to the Minister. It's a very good job.'

'I see. So you know this little corner very well?'

'Yes. Rudi and I bought this cottage. The Government put it up for sale two years ago. The Forest Supervisor lives in Baltz now and has a helicopter. We thought we'd use this as a holiday cottage. In fact we haven't used it, except for an occasional week-end. Last year we both went abroad.'

'Where did you go?' he asked, interested in her.

'I went to Obergurgl for a whole month in the winter. I never take summer holidays. During the summer I can relax in the sun every week-end. It's in winter that I want a break.'

'And so you went to Obergurgl.'

'Yes,' she chuckled. 'I saved hard and had a first class holiday, just like a rich girl. It was wonderful. Money was no object. Perhaps it sounds foolish, but I'll never forget that holiday as long as I live. I shan't do it again, but just for once it was nice to live in real luxury. This winter I'll come up here.' Then her face clouded. 'If I'm still in Carmania,' she added.

'I expect you will be. Don't look so gloomy. Tell me, where do you live now?'

'My mother died eight years ago, and Rudi and I went to stay with an aunt till we had finished at university and got jobs. Four years ago we bought a flat in the old part of Borgrad, and we share it. It's really two flats in one.'

'I didn't know Borgrad had an old part. I've never seen that.'

'You wouldn't, probably. You go out past the railway station, and it's on the far side of the industrial estate. The original Borgrad wasn't exactly where the present city is. Old Borgrad is about six kilometres from the city centre. It's all residential. Visitors rarely go there and of course all the important people live in the new city, but I like the old place. Our flat, for instance, is the upstairs part of a very old house and we have our own side entrance.'

'I see. Isn't it a bit awkward sharing with your brother? What about his girl friends and your boy friends?'

'You don't think I'd ask a man to the flat *alone*, do you?' she asked, staring.

'Um, no. Of course not. How silly of me.'

Wonders will never cease, he thought. She blushes, and she wouldn't ask a man to her flat. I wonder if her boy friend will have to ask her elder brother for permission to marry her. 'More coffee?' she offered.

'Let's make up a flask. Do you have a flask?'

'Yes, we brought two large ones with us. Just in case.'

'Sound planning,' Charles laughed. 'Let's fill one and you can take me along some of these woodland paths you know so well. I promise not to run away. I'll give you my parole. I just want to stretch my legs.'

'All right,' she agreed readily.

The truth was that she wanted to get

out too. Just being here at the old cottage brought back a host of memories of what had been an uncommonly happy childhood. So she made the coffee and put it and some biscuits and the gun into a basket, and they set off together. The cottage lay to the west of the mountain road which ran from Baltz, on the plain below, through Rindt and on until it emerged at the south-east corner of the boomerang-shaped Cascamite Range, at a place called Stephanschlag. To the north of the cottage was Rindt itself, with its rather difficult ski slopes. Elisabeth led the way along a leafy path which curved round to the south of the cottage. Their route lay among the trees, and in places the track was barely wide enough for single file. After about half an hour they came on a small clearing with a deep pool of clear, cold water.

'A tarn,' Charles exclaimed.

'What's a tarn?' she asked.

'That's what we call a pool like this in England, a mountain pool not fed by

72

a river. What a nice spot.'

'Rudi and I swam here sometimes, but it's very cold. Shall we have our coffee now?'

She unscrewed the double top of a flask and poured two mugs of coffee and they sat on a grassy hillock to drink it.

'Do you know,' Charles said suddenly, 'I'm enjoying myself.'

'Are you?' Elisabeth was surprised. 'Why? It's very quiet and dull here, and you've been kidnapped. I thought you'd hate it.'

'Well you see I spend most of my life rushing around the world. It's exhausting. Today I've got nothing to do except enjoy myself. I was going to go to Doppler next week for a week's holiday, but even that would have been a sort of treadmill — play golf twice a day, swim, perhaps play bridge in the evening. Always rushing from one thing to another. Here there is literally nothing to do. I can lie in the sun and just think; I can read, or sleep. I'm being well fed.

I've got good company and I'm not giving a single thought to business, because what good would it do? Yes, I like it. It's years since I've felt like this.'

'You're funny,' she laughed. 'How does it feel to be rich and important?'

'You don't feel it at all. You're too busy.'

'What a funny sort of life. I think I'd rather be poor. I have my evenings to myself, and weekends, and a month's holiday a year.'

'I've never taken a month a year, not since I left school anyway.'

'Why, Mr. Gresham?'

'Don't you think you'd better call me Charles if we're going to be forced to put up with each other for the next few days? Why, you asked — because my father wanted me to learn about his business. After all, it will be mine one day so I have to know all about it. I've had to work a lot harder than most of the twenty thousand men we employ.'

'Twenty thousand? Really?'

'Yes, mostly in Germany but some in

Britain and some in America. Soon there'll be more in Carmania.'

'Do you enjoy it?'

'Enjoy what?' he asked.

'Having to worry about twenty thousand men. Having no time off.'

Charles thought about that. *Did* he enjoy it? He rarely thought consciously about enjoyment.

'I suppose I must do, but this makes a nice change.'

'Is your father really a millionaire?'

'I suppose so. It all depends on what you mean by a millionaire. He hasn't got a million pounds in the bank. I shouldn't think anyone has. It's all in stocks and shares. He draws a salary from the group just like the rest of us.'

'Oh, is that all?'

Charles laughed. It was difficult explaining just what was involved in being rich. The ordinary person imagined an inexhaustible bank account, but it wasn't quite like that.

'Look here,' he said, 'take my case. It's easier to explain. I've got a quarter of a million in shares. My father gave it to me. I don't get any income from it because I use my dividends to buy more shares. So my share capital is growing all the time, but remember I pay pretty heavy taxes on my dividends. What I live on is my salary which is fifty thousand pounds a year.'

'Sterling! Fifty thousand *sterling*?' She squeaked the words incredulously.

'Yes, but my income tax is about seventy per cent. That leaves less than eighteen thousand — hardly enough to buy a new Rolls-Royce. I have a Rolls-Royce, but it belongs to the company. I have a beautiful big country house too, but it belongs to the company as well and I pay rent to live in it.'

'Oh dear, I don't understand.'

'I know, hardly anybody does. It's all very complicated.'

'It seems to me,' Elisabeth said slowly, 'that I own more than you do. Rudi and I own the flat between us, and this cottage between us, and we each have our own cars. You don't even have a car of your own.'

'Can't afford one. I daren't be seen in anything less than a Rolls, and you won't catch me paying out more than fourteen thousand of my own money on anything so sordid as a means of locomotion.'

'I think you're pulling my leg,' she told him suspiciously.

'Not a bit of it. Of course I travel first class all over the world, I stay in the best suites in the best hotels, I dine à la carte — most of all that is on expenses. I hardly ever see Tabarie.'

'Tabarie?'

'My house in Gloucestershire, about a mile from my father's house. You see I only spend about five months of the year in England. I spend most of the rest in Germany where we made all our money after the war. My father was in the Allied Control Commission, and he took his demobilisation in Germany and started up a business there.'

'Why did he do that?'

77

'Because he is a very astute man. He saw that Germany was going to work night and day to restore its economy. It was simple to start up a factory in his time — everything was so cheap, nobody had any money. He had a little and borrowed more to start up his first factory. We have fifteen factories in Germany now, six in Britain, three in America, and we hope to start one here.'

'Help!' Elisabeth said weakly. 'What a man he must be, this father of yours.'

'He's rather splendid,' Charles agreed, thinking of his distinguished and handsome parent with the white mane of hair and the white moustache that gave the immediate impression that he was an Ambassador, if not someone even more important.

'Couldn't you just let other people run the factories, and sell all your shares and things, and live on the interest?'

'Yes, I suppose we could. Selling the shares would be tricky — we wouldn't want to start a panic on the stock market — but we could pull out of the business and live on income.'

'Would you have a lot of money?'

'Enough to make the income tax people dance with joy.'

'Then why not do that and enjoy your life?'

'Who said I'm not enjoying it?' Charles countered.

'You can't possibly be. I mean, I had a month in a small suite in the most expensive hotel in Obergurgl. It was fantastic. I saved for two years for that holiday. I loved it. But I'd hate to do it for two months. That's no way to live. I'm going to marry a farmer and live in the country.'

'Oh are you? Which farmer?' Charles asked bleakly.

'I don't know. I haven't picked one yet,' she laughed.

'Ah, I understand.'

For some ridiculous reason he felt better.

4

That handsome and distinguished business tycoon, Nigel Gresham, was as near to being distraught as anyone had ever seen him. When he received the bad news at his house in Eaton Square he leapt into action. In no time at all he had sent a cable to Prime Minister Jung, booked a seat on the first flight out, ordered his town Rolls to the ready position, galvanised his valet into packing for him, and treated his gracious and long-suffering wife to a lengthy diatribe on the folly of providing free education for university students who were nothing but embryonic gangsters. The fact that it probably wasn't students who had abducted his only son was immaterial. Students would do.

Shortly before he left in great haste to sort out matters in Carmania, the telephone rang. Nigel picked it up fully expecting to hear one of his higher paid minions explain that there was a slight problem. They were like children who needed wet nursing. Instead he heard a female voice.

'Mr. Gresham, it's Janice.'

'Oh. Oh, Janice.' He put his hand over the mouthpiece and called to his wife, who had heard perfectly clearly, 'It's Janice.'

He scowled as he spoke. Janice Innescourt was thirty and unmarried. She was very beautiful indeed, an out and out thoroughbred, whose father was currently High Sheriff for Gloucestershire, as of course one would expect of the contemporary Innescourt of Ferndown Court, near Cirencester. Janice was beautiful, talented, moderately well off, knew everybody — and was an out and out snob. Currently she also happened to be in love with Charles Gresham.

'Are you there, Mr. Gresham?'

'Yes Janice. I'm on the point of leaving for the airport. I'm going to

Carmania to bring Charles home.'

'They've found him?' she asked blankly.

'No, of course not, the nincompoops. He's been kidnapped.'

'I know, that's why I telephoned.'

'Well, don't you worry yourself about that. I'm going to Borgrad now, and I'll soon get some action out of those layabouts there. Imagine anyone being kidnapped in a sleepy little hole like Borgrad!'

'I've never been there.'

'Neither have I, but I got reports on it before I sent Charles off.'

'Is there anything I can do?' Janice offered gallantly.

Nigel considered this. She was an excellent horsewoman and a splendid hostess, especially on formal occasions. As he was not planning a cavalry charge or an eve of Waterloo ball, she had not much to offer.

'No thanks. We must wait and see what happens.'

'Mrs. Gresham must be most distressed. Would you like me to come up to Town to be with her while you're away?'

Nigel swallowed. The thought of inflicting Janice on his darling Nancy was almost too much for him. Nancy might look gracious, and live in opulent surroundings, but she remained very stubbornly the amusing, down-to-earth girl who had once been his Commanding Officer's youngest daughter. The penniless Army brat had nothing in common with an Innescourt who had an overdeveloped sense of her importance. Indeed, neither Nigel nor Nancy knew why Charles encouraged the wretched girl.

'I don't think so, thank you. It's very kind of you to offer, very kind, but Nancy would rather be left alone at a time like this,' he lied gallantly.

Nancy, who was listening with interest, gave him a grateful smile. A few moments later he hung up.

'You heard. She wanted to come here and hold your hand.'

'I guessed. Thank you for sparing me.

The car is waiting,' she told him.

'Then I must be off.' He kissed his wife tenderly. 'I'll telephone every evening of course and whenever there's any news. You mustn't worry, Nancy. Charles can look after himself. He's tough.'

His wife gave him an amused smile. 'I never thought I'd live to see this day,' she told him.

'What day? Charles being kidnapped?'

'No, I'm sure that's all a silly mistake. They'll let him go. I mean you and Charles both away in a place like Borgrad. Who's going to run the empire?'

'Devil take the empire,' he snapped impatiently. 'No time to worry about that.'

He kissed her again, wondering what had got into her, and hurried out to the waiting Rolls. Three hours later Belmont's man in Frankfurt, who had rushed to Borgrad, met his chief at the airport with a hired Mercedes 600 limousine.

'Your hotel suite is arranged sir,' he said with noticeable deference.

'Never mind about that. Tell the driver to take me to the Prime Minister.'

'You have an appointment for this afternoon at three, sir . . . '

'That's no good,' Nigel snapped. 'I want to see Jung now, then the police chief, whoever he might be. Tell the driver.'

Much to the harassed Frankfurt managing director's astonishment, Nigel Gresham succeeded in interrupting Bruno Jung's morning. He listened to an account of what had been going on, asked a great many questions, informed the Prime Minister in no uncertain terms that his son had better be found, and that very soon, and then was whisked off to cross-examine Heinrich Braun who had been receiving depressingly negative reports from his helicopter and road patrols and from the army and police detachments who had already begun to comb the country.

While Nigel Gresham was rushing about, impeding those who were trying to help, and totally oblivious to what might be going on in the industrial empire which he had created almost by accident, Charles and Elisabeth were walking slowly back to the cottage. It seemed quite natural that they should walk hand in hand, and Charles — nothing if not a considerate man, was carrying the basket in which, incidentally, lay the gun which both of them had forgotten.

Charles was aware of the stirring of many strange emotions this sunny summer's morning. He was in equilibrium, as it were, rushing neither hither nor thither, and this in itself gave him an unusual sense of peace. He had slept like a baby, eaten a hearty breakfast, spent the morning in the company of an extremely attractive girl, and not once had he had to discuss or even consider business.

Suddenly they became aware of a beating sound and they stopped and listened. After a second or two Charles said, 'Helicopters. Let's just move over to the side of the path among those bushes.'

'All right.'

She led the way and they stood among some bushes, under an overhang of trees, and looked up at the ribbon of sky overhead. The noise increased and then it came into view, a blue and white police helicopter. They could see an observer peering down at the ground, searching; then it was gone.

'Quite a fuss you've stirred up,' Charles remarked as they continued their journey.

'It will be time for the news when we get back. We'll listen before I make lunch.'

'What are we having today?'

'Salad, unless you'd prefer something cooked.'

'No, salad is fine.'

'I forgot to tell you last night, but we got in some drinks in case you'd like them. There's whisky and gin and some sherry.'

'I'm afraid I never touch the stuff.'

'Don't you? Oh well, Rudi can have it. I thought I'd mention it. If you want anything, just ask.'

'Who's paying for all this?' Charles demanded.

'There's nothing much to pay for, except food and drink, and Rudi and I provided that. Some of our friends helped out with extra bedding and things.'

'How many of there are you in this, Elisabeth?'

'I don't think I should tell you that. Not many — just a few friends.'

'I've seen four of you so far. What's happened to the other two?'

'They've gone away. Rudi and I will guard you by ourselves.'

'That's very nice for me, but why?'

'We wouldn't like you to be able to identify the others.'

'So you and Rudi are taking all the risks?'

'We have to, don't we?'

'It was your idea, wasn't it?' he asked.

'Yes. How did you know?'

'I guessed — something in your manner.'

'Why did you say it was very nice for you . . . that Rudi and I were guarding you ourselves?' she asked.

'Well . . . I don't have to get used to new faces all the time. I can get to know you both properly. It's much cosier this way.'

'Cosy. What a funny word to use.'

She flashed him a quick smile and he squeezed her hand — all in a purely platonic manner, needless to say. A moment or two later they arrived back at the cottage. Elisabeth switched on the radio and they sat down to listen.

Soon the news began.

'There is still no news of Charles Gresham, the missing businessman who was kidnapped yesterday afternoon by a gang of terrorists who want the Government to cancel the defence treaty with America, allowing the Americans to build one or more atomic missile bases in this country. A full scale search has been mounted by the police and the army, and all the helicopters in the country are being used.

'In a letter delivered to the Prime Minister yesterday evening the kidnappers threatened that unless the defence treaty is cancelled within three days, Mr. Gresham will be killed, and that further acts of terrorism would then follow. The person who delivered the letter was not seen.

'Mr. Nigel Gresham, founder of Belmont Industries International, and father of the missing businessman, arrived in Borgrad by air a short time ago. He has had meetings with the Prime Minister and the Chief of Police. Mr. Nigel Gresham built up the large business of which his son is presently chairman, and the company is proposing to establish a factory in Carmania which would provide employment for approximately two thousand people.

'In an interview just before this bulletin began, Mr. Gresham said he would stay in Carmania until his son was found. Asked if he considered that his son's life was in danger, Mr. Gresham stated that while violence could not be ruled out, he hoped that the police would trace his son quickly and release him. He said that his plans for a factory in Carmania were not at present affected by events.

'Mr. Jason McCudden, the American Ambassador who, it is believed was the victim originally chosen by the kidnappers, has left by air for Washington for talks with the U.S. Government on the defence agreement. Prime Minister Jung told press, radio and television reporters in a special press conference this morning that the defence agreement has been signed and is now official. There is at present no question of cancelling it. The kidnapping was undoubtedly the work of irresponsible and hysterical people who possibly believed that they were acting for the good of their country. In answer to a question he stated that it was not believed to be the work of any student body, and that Carmanian students had always shown themselves to be sensible and responsible people. The students had made one demonstration on the defence agreement issue, but it had been peaceful and orderly.'

When the news was finished Charles whistled quietly.

'Father's here. He must be worried.'

'Well he would be. That's natural,' Elisabeth remarked.

'I suppose so. I'm sorry for your Prime Minister if my father has decided to take a hand in matters personally. The poor man will never know a moment's peace till I turn up.'

'We are causing you a lot of trouble,' Elisabeth apologised.

'You know what they say — you can't make an omelette without breaking eggs. If it gets you what you want, you should be satisfied.'

'*If* it does,' she agreed ruefully. 'I wonder if it will. What do you think of the defence agreement, Charles?'

'I think that on the whole it's

probably a good thing. I'm all in favour of disarmament, in principle, but it's impossible to get anyone to start it. Everyone's scared. So, as long as things are as they are, I think the missile bases are probably for the best. On the other hand it's not my country, remember, and I haven't thought about it a lot. Your point of view may very well be the better one.'

'I expected you would fume and shout and demand to be released.'

'If I did, would you let me go?'

'No.'

'Then there's no point, is there? You have got a problem, haven't you?'

'Which problem?' she asked.

'What will you do on Monday if they haven't cancelled the agreement? *They* may think you're going to kill me. They don't know who you are. I do, and I don't believe for one second you or your brother would kill anyone or anything. So you may be in a spot.'

'We'll just have to wait and see what happens.' Then her eyes opened wide.

'If you believe I wouldn't shoot you, why don't you run away?'

'It's much too warm a day for running,' Charles replied lightly.

★ ★ ★

Janice Innescourt was tall and dark, beautifully groomed and expensively dressed. She was the only child of a very old family indeed, and her parents were understandably anxious to see her married and the mother of a son to carry on the family tradition and to inherit Ferndown Court, one of Gloucestershire's more stately piles. Charles Gresham was the ideal answer; for although nobody knew just where the Greshams had come from — other than the fact that Nigel had been a Major in the army in World War Two — Charles had been to a good public school and was immensely rich. To keep Ferndown Court going, money would be needed, more than Sir Godwin Innescourt, twelfth and last baronet, was going to leave to his daughter.

It was one of the wonders of Ferndown Court that anyone so shapely and beautiful to behold as Janice should have remained unmarried for so long. There had been no lack of suitable young men in the circle in which the family moved, but somehow none of them ever reached the point of voicing the crucial question. There had been a positively ominous lack of 'Wilt thou's', as though the poor girl had one of the more extreme forms of body odour or galloping halitosis. Needless to say she had neither, being well provided with expensive toiletries to prevent such catastrophes.

Then Charles had appeared on the scene. He had bought Tabarie, near Kemble, and restored the house and moved in. Unfortunately he spent most of his time away from the place, but he had contrived to meet Janice early on, and they had become an accepted twosome. She had gone up to Town several times to go to shows with him, and he never came to Gloucestershire without calling at Ferndown Court.

It was obvious he must be serious, but he too seemed to be stricken with some dire malady which prevented him from putting The Question. Now that her thirtieth birthday was three months behind her, Janice was becoming quite desperate and would probably even have considered some wretched R.A.F. officer living on his pay, had it not been for her conviction that dear Charles was simply shy. So far she had not found a way to cure his shyness.

Now, however, she perceived her golden opportunity. Without telling her parents what precisely she had in mind, she drove to London in order to get the evening flight to Frankfurt and then Borgrad. By now the story of the kidnapped tycoon was all the talk in the City, so when she telephoned a certain television personality and informed him that she, who was engaged to marry the missing Charles, was on her way to Borgrad to pray for his safe deliverance, a human interest story was scented.

When Dickie Knight heard all the details — a baronet who was also High Sheriff, a stately home, a simply stunning girl who was only too delighted to answer questions, and who was actually engaged to the missing man — he knew that he had his topical story for that night. The interview lasted seven minutes, which was a very long time indeed, but Janice was worth it.

Janice then departed for Borgrad, purring with pleasure, secure in the knowledge that fifty-five and a half-million people in Great Britain — and more, in other parts of the world in due course — *knew* that Charles Gresham was engaged to the lovely Miss Innescourt. Had it not said so on telly? Let Charles wriggle his way out of that, she thought. Of course, when he was finally unearthed in Borgrad and produced in front of the press and television people there, his fiancée would be by his side. He'd jolly well have to marry her now. Her father would be proud of her. It was not by mere fluke that the Innescourts had survived the centuries, firmly entrenched in their stately home. Their instinct for survival was strong and did not desert them in an emergency.

Nigel Gresham had finished dinner, and actually found himself at a loose end that evening. He could not concentrate on the affairs of Belmont Industries, which in truth managed very well by themselves. He found Carmanian television incredibly dull, and although he was fluent in German, he found it tiring after a time also. There was nothing of interest in the magazine he had bought, and he had despatched the Frankfurt managing director back to his post with suitable thanks for arranging car, driver, hotel and various other things such as money, and so on. Now he sat in the bar and drank tomato juice and brooded. What was the use of it all, he wondered? He'd gone into business in Germany after the war with a good deal of zest. He had been in his early thirties then and anxious to make a little money.

He sighed and signalled for more tomato juice. He'd spent the past quarter-century amassing wealth which he couldn't even begin to spend, he had neglected his very lovable wife on numerous occasions, and now his only child, his son, the apple of his eye, was in danger. If anything happened to Charles — perish the thought, but they *had* said they'd kill him — all his success would be as ashes. He reflected on the time he had wasted. He and Charles could have gone fishing, taken holidays together, played golf with one another, done all sorts of things — but they had both been too busy. They never seemed to be free at the same time. They only met to discuss business. They hadn't even spent Christmas together for years. Better a second-hand Rolls and a flat to the west of Belgravia — say in South Ken — if you could be with your family and be happy.

He was conscious of the fact that he

was sixty-two. Only thirty-eight years to go till he got his centenary telegram from Buck House, after which he might well die. Time was growing short. If he got Charles back — correction, *when* he got Charles back — he would devote more time to him. The poor boy was working too hard. They'd go to Scotland, that's what. September in Scotland was nice, they said. Nancy would like it too. A whole month together, just the three of them. To blazes with Belmont Industries. All he'd ever wanted was one reasonably prosperous factory, and not too much income tax; but somehow it seemed you had to keep going in order to survive. It was ridiculous. Yes, and Charles could find himself a girl, a nice sensible girl like his mother, not one of those ghastly snobs like that Innescourt girl. Then there would be a grandson, a Nigel the Second.

He drank his tomato juice with reckless abandon and ordered more. Who cared? Fill it up! He'd have a

word with that Prime Minister fellow,
now, this minute. He'd tell him that if
he didn't tear up that defence agreement, Belmont Industries would pull
out of America lock stock and barrel
and keep out of Carmania to. They
would wage bloody and unceasing war
on Carmania. In addition Nigel Gresham would broadcast loud and far the
fact that the Prime Minister of
Carmania was a heartless bureaucrat,
willing to sacrifice human lives in order
to get into an arms race with countries
which could swallow up Carmania and
never notice it. He would write to the
Grand Duke Philip, ruler of Carmania,
at present in the neighbouring country
of Baratavia where he had just got
himself engaged to Princess Fiona-
Alina, heir to the Baratavian crown. He
would, in short, do anything and
everything he could to make life
unpleasant for Bruno Jung personally.

Before he could put his plan into
effect, two men accosted him in the bar.
They were from the television company.

Cameras were being set up in the foyer. Would Mr. Gresham please co-operate?

'In what way?' Nigel demanded.

'Your son's fiancée has just arrived at the airport and is on her way here to join you in your lonely vigil,' said a young man who was poetically inclined.

'What did you say? My son's *what*?'

'The young noblewoman to whom he is engaged.' Nigel's eyes popped at that while the man consulted his notebook. 'Miss Janice Innescourt whose father is Sir Innescourt, Sheriff of England.' Nigel choked. 'We did not know that your son was engaged to be married. If you would just allow us to film you meeting your future daughter-in-law?'

Nigel swallowed his tomato juice in a gulp.

'I . . . er . . . she's here, did you say?'

'Yes, she is on her way. She will be here in a few moments. She arrived unexpectedly. We have interviewed her at the airport. Earlier this evening she was interviewed in London by . . . ' his voice dropped an octave in homage

. . . 'by Mr. Dickie Knight.'

'You don't say.'

'Indeed yes. If you would please come this way . . . '

For once dazed and at a loss, Nigel allowed himself to be steered to the foyer where the hotel manager and some of the guests regarded him with that special reverence reserved for people lucky enough to be chased by television cameras — T.V.I.Ps, as Nigel often called them scathingly.

He managed to control his temper during the brief scene which followed almost at once, but he followed Janice to her room in due course and scowled when she smiled sweetly.

'Just when did you and Charles become engaged?' he demanded.

'On my birthday,' she lied shamelessly. 'We were keeping it a secret. We were going to announce it on your wedding anniversary. It seemed such a nice idea.' This inspiration had come to her in the aircraft because she had anticipated that Nigel might be uncouth enough to demand details of the engagement. 'Of course it is different now. Now that dear Charles is in trouble I must stand by him. I can't turn my back on him by pretending we are not engaged,' she concluded with a dignity which would have secured her a two hundred dollar a week contract for a supporting role in a Hollywood B picture.

'I see.' Nigel was in no position to contradict this. He would discuss it with Charles later. He did not intend to spend a month in Scotland if Janice Innescourt were coming along. 'Well I hope you'll be comfortable. You must excuse me. I have to telephone the Prime Minister.'

'Because I'm here?' Janice asked, open-eyed.

'No. Something else. I'll see you tomorrow.'

Nigel stomped from the room, but much of the fire had gone from him. When he spoke to Jung, after some difficulty, he forgot to bluster. Afterwards he found the night reporter from the local newspaper waiting hopefully. He took that young man into the bar and told him exactly why Carmania must tear up the defence agreement, and finally retired to bed exhausted and bewildered by the gamut of his emotions.

5

They sat together on the rather lumpy settee, drinking coffee and listening to some light music on the radio. Rudi was out, making a telephone call.

'You never answered my question, Charles,' Elisabeth said suddenly. 'I asked you why you don't just go away if you don't believe we'd harm you. During the day when Rudi's asleep you could just walk out. I could hardly stop you. Even Rudi might find it difficult, although he's taller than you are.'

Charles turned and looked at her thoughtfully. 'I don't know how to explain. When you kidnapped me I thought those guns were real. Then that first night, as I got to know you a little better, I wondered. You are the least bloodthirsty gang of kidnappers anyone can imagine. The whole thing was so amateur that I had a look at a gun. It's a beautiful model, and it must have cost between ten and fifteen pounds. I've heard of them, exactly like a real one. People buy that sort of thing nowadays — collectors and so on. Then I thought about everything. I had a long talk to Rudi — goodness, was it only last night? — and there was a long talk with you today. I think you ought to have a chance to overthrow your defence agreement. Just for once I'd like to see the little people win. You see, in real life they never do. It's always the big battalions that win life's battles. I find my feelings hard to explain.'

'You're on our side?' she asked incredulously.

'I'm not on anybody's side as far as the agreement itself is concerned, but if you and your friends are so worked up about it, and you want to do something, then good luck to you. If those guns were real it would be different — I'd get away somehow. Does any of that make sense?'

'Not very much — except that I think you are nice.'

'Do you?' He wondered when he had last heard anyone say that to him. Janice, who wanted to marry him, would consider such a direct personal remark as the infallible sign of a lower class upbringing.

'Well, I daresay the holiday will do me good. I told you this morning, I'm actually enjoying myself. It's you I'm worried about.'

Her peal of laughter startled him. She explained.

'It's so funny. We have kidnapped you and threatened your life, and *you* are worried about us!'

'It is a bit odd, isn't it? It must be middle age approaching.'

'You look young.'

'I'm thirty-six. How old are you?'

'Twenty-six.'

'You're just a child. When I'm eighty you'll only be seventy,' he told her.

She laughed. 'When I'm a hundred you'll be an old man of a hundred and ten,' she agreed.

It must be the surroundings or the weather or something, Charles thought. I'm enjoying this inane conversation. He wondered when he had last really *enjoyed* conversation. It was nice to clinch a business deal, but that was triumph rather than enjoyment.

'We'll have to make plans,' he said. 'I bet they won't give in. What we really ought to do is sneak over the border, get a plane to England and go to my country house in Gloucestershire. We'd be safe there, and you and Rudi could take photographs of me all tied up and gagged, with one of you wearing a hood and pointing a gun at me, and send them to Jung. Nobody would ever find us, because Tabarie is the last place they'd look. We could stay there for weeks and I could write pathetic little notes in a shaky hand saying that I'm dying of starvation and malnutrition.'

They giggled. 'It wouldn't work of course. No passport, so how would I get to England? Anyway there would be

British stamps on the envelopes. We'll have to think of something else.'

'Do you always talk nonsense?' she asked.

'No, hardly ever. It's a pleasant change for me. You know, you're very pretty.'

'I expect you say that to a lot of girls.'

'I've really only said it to one, and she isn't nearly as nice a person as you are, though she's pretty enough.'

'I don't believe you. You're probably married.'

'Not a bit of it,' he denied. 'Not even engaged. I'm free, white and a little over twenty-one.'

'Why is it someone so wealthy isn't married? Plenty of girls would want you.'

'I don't meet very many girls, and none I'd like to marry. I've never really taken time off, you see. Would you marry me, Elisabeth?'

'I don't think that's very funny.'

He looked crestfallen. 'No, I suppose not. To you I'm just a middle-aged foreigner. I think I'll go to bed if you don't mind. Shall we go walking again tomorrow?'

'Yes, if you wish, Charles,'

'I'd like it a lot. We're stuck with one another, so we might as well make the most of it. Say goodnight to Rudi for me. I was awake late last night and I really must catch up with my sleep.'

'All right. Anything I can get you before you go to bed?'

'No, nothing thanks.'

He went into the bedroom and a few minutes later she heard water running in the bathroom. Rudi wandered in and looked all round.

'Where's Charles?' he asked.

'He's gone to bed, Rudi. He says he's tired. Do you know, he actually wants us to succeed? He knows the guns are dummies.'

'*What*? How do you know that?'

'He told me. He could get away from here any time he wants.'

'Is that so?' Rudi glowered. 'Then why does he stay?'

His sister told him and he listened, not quite understanding.

'I think I'd better go into Rindt and telephone,' he said at last. 'Just to be on the safe side. Now that we've gone to all this trouble, we don't want him suddenly deciding to walk out. I mean, the whole police force and the army and everyone has been turned out to look for us, and there are helicopters buzzing everywhere. Now his father has flown from England. Liz, if they catch us, they'll crucify us.'

'They will, won't they? What are you telephoning for?'

'I'll get Willi to bring up a shotgun and some ammunition from the farm.'

'No!'

'Yes. What's more, just to show Charles it works, I'll shoot something for his breakfast in the morning.'

'What's the point? You'd never shoot *him* with a shotgun, Rudi.'

'I bet he won't put it to the test.'

She could not talk him out of it. He went off and telephoned, and Willie promised to drive up in the middle of the night. While Rudi was out, Elisabeth thought about their prisoner. He seemed very friendly, very friendly indeed. Was he flirting with her, or did he really like her? It was strange that they should have become such friends. If it hadn't been for the kidnapping, they'd never even have met because they moved in entirely different worlds.

She was not dissatisfied with her life — she enjoyed it a great deal. She had no hankering for formal balls, big glittering cars, huge houses or any of the trappings of wealth. It was nice to be able to have a good holiday occasionally, to be waited on hand and foot for a week or two, but it was even nicer to do things oneself. She decided she'd take Charles out in the morning before breakfast to pick mushrooms, and they could come back and fry them in butter. Great big piles of mushrooms, with some bacon and eggs — but mostly mushrooms. That would be a lovely breakfast, and no mush-rooms tasted as nice as the ones you picked yourself first thing after you got out of bed. She'd bet he'd never picked a mushroom in his life.

It was up to her to show him all the things he was missing. When this business was over he'd go back to his factories, conference rooms, hotel life; but sometimes he would stop for a second or two amid all his rushing and remember the woods and the flowers and fresh mushrooms for breakfast. That would be nice for him.

Just before Rudi came back from the village she switched on the radio, which had been silent for the past half-hour. The timing was exact. Almost at once a voice said:

'We interrupt this programme to bring you a special news bulletin on the missing British businessman. Earlier this evening Miss Janice Innescourt, who is engaged to marry Mr. Charles Gresham, kidnapped yesterday outside the American Embassy in Borgrad, arrived at Borgrad airport. Miss Innescourt, who is twenty-five, is the daughter of Sir Godwin and Lady Innescourt, of Ferndown Court in Gloucestershire, England. Sir Godwin is the High Sheriff of Gloucestershire. Miss Innescourt told reporters at the airport that she had flown to Borgrad to share Mr. Nigel Gresham's vigil. Mr. Gresham, father of the missing man, arrived earlier today.

'Miss Innescourt was driven from the airport to her hotel where she was met by Mr. Gresham. It is understood that they will both remain in the country until Mr. Charles Gresham is released by the kidnappers.

'In an interview later this evening, Mr. Nigel Gresham said that he has informed Prime Minister Jung that it is his duty to cancel the defence agreement with the United States. 'My son's life is worth more than any sordid armaments agreement' Mr. Gresham said, 'I have cabled the Secretary General of the United Nations, and also Grand Duke Philip who is at present in Baratavia, and I appeal to all decent thinking people to add their voices to mine. We have only two more days to go before my son will be ruthlessly murdered by these fiends, and all because of a squalid arms deal. It is not only my son's life which is at stake, but international peace.'

'Mr. Gresham is the founder of the Belmont Industries International group of companies in Germany, Britain and America. Although the group owns a great many companies, it does not deal in arms, ammunition or high explosives, Mr. Gresham stated.

'The Prime Minister tonight refused to make any comment on Mr. Gresham's demand that the agreement be ended, but Chief of Police Heinrich Braun said it was only a matter of time now till Mr. Charles Gresham is rescued and his abductors are brought to trial.'

Elisabeth got up and switched off the set. She walked to the doorway and stood staring blindly out into the velvety darkness. Why had he lied to her, she asked herself? Why? He said he had never been engaged, and all the time he was engaged to some society girl in England, someone whose father was a Sir. What a stupid little country cousin he must think her. Pick his own mushrooms indeed. Sweet memories to brighten his life in quieter moments! Rubbish. Nonsense. He was a nasty, calculating liar, pretending to be a friend.

When Rudi returned three or four minutes later she had wiped away the few tears.

'Did you get the gun?' she asked briskly.

'No, of course not. I only went to telephone Willi. He'll bring the gun in a couple of hours.'

'Good. I hope you remembered to ask for plenty of ammunition. We may need it.'

He stared at his sister, wondering what had brought about this change.

Charles awoke and lay in bed blinking as the sunlight streamed into the room. He had slept like the proverbial baby and felt wonderfully refreshed. This was indeed the life he had been missing for years without realising it. He sat up, stretched, and then examined his clothes. His shirt was a little grubby, and his trousers no longer had that natty appearance on which he prided himself. It didn't matter much about the dark grey trousers, but a clean shirt would be nice. He must ask Rudi about it. After all he had about a hundred pounds in Carmanian marks in his wallet. He might as well use it. The problem was where to get the shirt?

He went to the bathroom and washed and shaved, and then dressed. As he did so he was thinking of Elisabeth Renner. Twenty-six was such a good age — old enough to be mature and yet delightfully young . . . and beautiful. She had silky dark hair that suited her so well, and startling blue eyes. When she smiled there was just the merest hint of a dimple in one cheek. Right or left? Right. Yes, that was it. Looking back over the years it seemed that almost all the women he had met had either been rich and bored, or else efficient and boring, depending on whether he knew them socially or in business. Here was an honest-to-God ordinary girl — no, not ordinary, that was an injustice. Ordinary perhaps in the sense that she was human, feminine, natural, and unpretentious, and all the other things he liked. None the less a graduate, a very pretty girl and above all one who was prepared to kidnap an ambassador in what she thought was a just cause. Definitely not ordinary.

He was humming a little as he finished knotting the laces of his shoes. They needed cleaning, he noted. Clean shoes, neat tidy hair, pressed trousers — these things were important to him. A man who didn't take pride in his appearance wouldn't take pride in his work either. His mother had taught him that, and when all was said and done his mother was generally correct. He didn't approve of the Shirley Temples who worked in his companies, the long haired youths, but provided they were clean and neat, he said nothing.

He had another hasty look in the mirror. He didn't actually look thirty-six. He didn't really look much older than Elisabeth. At least he didn't think so. He opened the door and went into the living room. He could hear her in the kitchen and he went in after her.

'Good morning, good morning,' he said cheerfully. 'What a fetching sight you are in a nice clean apron. What's for breakfast today, Elisabeth?'

'Fried eggs and bacon,' she answered, curtly.

'Good, good. By jove, I slept well. Like a baby. I feel fine this morning. Breakfast soon?'

'I'm doing my best. I started when I heard you in the bathroom.'

'I'm not complaining, just asking,' he said, blinking. 'Where's Rudi? Did he miss me last night?'

'I shouldn't think so. He's got other interests you know. He's gone for the newspaper.'

There was a chill about the whole episode which he could not help noticing. She did not look at him. She mumbled her words as though she didn't want to speak to him either. And that was no way to fry eggs.

He wandered out until she called him, and he saw that she had laid his place for breakfast on the kitchen table. Yesterday it had been at the dining table in the dining area of the living room. He shrugged sat down . . . and then stared. Two eggs with burnt bottoms, some shrivelled bacon, and a lot of grease. The toast had been cut too thin, and was all bent and twisted like a decayed leaf. If you dished up food like this in Pentonville the prisoners would telephone the union and call a general strike. He didn't know what was wrong, but he was intelligent enough to know when someone was indicating that he could go to hell.

He picked up his plate and the toast rack and went to the dustbin and tipped in the contents. Then he rummaged in the cupboards until he found what he wanted and patiently began to cook his own breakfast. Elisabeth said nothing. She sat on a kitchen stool and watched.

'Hullo,' he said suddenly. 'What's that in your hand?'

'A shotgun. It's loaded. Both barrels.'

'How bloody jolly. Sorry I asked.'

He resumed his cooking. When it was ready he sat down and ate his breakfast. Elisabeth had to admit that he had made a very workmanlike job of preparing it. That had surprised her. She didn't think he'd know how, but plainly at some stage or other of his life he'd been taught how to make breakfast. She compressed her lips. It did not matter.

Rudi burst in a few minutes later, excited.

'You should see the paper,' he said, waving it about. 'The newspaper office has been inundated with letters. Over a thousand they say, and every one begging the Government to cancel the agreement and save Charles's life. Isn't it fantastic? You should read that leader. There's also a fantastic interview with your father, Charles. He's sent cables to the United Nations and to Grand Duke Philip demanding that they intervene and have that agreement scrapped.'

'He has?' Charles asked disbelievingly.

'Yes. You read it for yourself. You too, Elisabeth. This is fantastic.' He didn't seem to be able to think of another word in his excitement. 'Oh,' he added carelessly, flinging the paper down and going over to the stove, 'there's rather a nice photograph of your fiancée, Charles.'

He looked at Elisabeth. 'Aren't you going to make me some breakfast Liz, before I get some sleep?'

'Yes.'

'Hey,' Charles interrupted. 'Photograph of *whom* did you say? Where?'

'Your fiancée. Inside front page.'

Charles turned to the page in a daze and gazed astonished at a large and rather nice picture of Janice Innescourt.

'But I haven't got a fiancée,' he said in a quiet voice.

'You have now,' Rudi chuckled. 'Take a look at her, Liz, she's a real film star.'

'She's a . . . ' Charles shut up. He remembered in time that he was supposed to be a gentleman. He read the paper carefully — all about Janice, his father, the search, and everything that related to himself. Then he got up and walked to the front door. Hastily Elisabeth thrust the gun into Rudi's hand.

'Guard him while I finish making your breakfast.'

'For goodness sake, where do you think he's going to go?' Rudi demanded.

'Do as I say.'

He shrugged and followed Charles, who was standing in the doorway staring outside.

'Something wrong, Charles?'

'Yes, quite a lot.'

'What's the bad news?' Rudi asked innocently.

'Have you got a girl friend, Rudi?'

'Yes.'

'Well take my advice and drop her. Women are pure hell.'

'But . . . your fiancée has come all this way just to be near you,' Rudi said, more puzzled than ever.

'She isn't my fiancée. This is a trick to make me marry her. She isn't twenty-five either, she's thirty,' he added ungallantly.

'You do know her, don't you? It says she was met by your father.'

'I know her all right. She was my girl friend for a time, but when I got to know her better . . . well, she isn't my type, that's all. The trouble is that I live quite near to them in the country and I see a lot of them when I'm at my country house. I know she was angling to marry me. In fact I'd decided to steer clear of her for the next six months or so. Now she's trapped me.'

'You mean she said you were engaged when you weren't?' Rudi laughed. 'That's funny. You don't have to marry her, do you?'

'I certainly won't, but now I've got to get rid of her.' He was thinking of Elisabeth as he spoke. No wonder he had been given canteen food for breakfast. He'd told her he was not engaged. Then he remembered that Rudi hadn't arrived with the paper until after the revolting plateful. There must be something else after all. He sighed. It was such a nice morning outside.

'What's the shotgun for?' he asked abruptly.

'Well,' Rudi coloured, 'Liz told me you knew the other guns were dummies. They belong to a friend of mine who . . . no, I'd better not talk about that. Anyway, when Liz said you could walk off whenever you want, I rang a friend and asked him to bring up a shotgun and some ammunition. It's nothing personal,' he said apologetically, 'but we have got rather a lot at stake here. I wouldn't want you to walk off.'

'I see.'

Charles was silent as he considered things. Suddenly it was all wrong, the pleasure had gone from life — the newfound pleasure which had begun to mean so much to him in such a short space of time. Why he had even . . . he had even been thinking about Elisabeth Renner in a way he had not considered a girl for a very long time. How stupid. Now they had a shotgun. Well, they needn't worry, he wouldn't give them away. Meantime it was high time he put paid to Janice Innescourt's pretensions. Unless he was much mistaken his mother would be almost in tears. He made up his mind to go.

'I'll go and see if my breakfast is ready,' Rudi said, propping the gun beside the fireplace.

'Okay Rudi.'

Charles waited till Rudi had disappeared into the kitchen, and then he stepped outside. He ran very silently. A few seconds later he was out of sight, heading in what he hoped was the direction of the village of Rindt.

6

Charles was on the correct path. He walked quickly, and stopped every now and then to listen. There was still no sound of pursuit. He hurried on until he came within sight of the village. He halted in the middle of the track and considered. Now that he was here, what should he do? Hire a car was the obvious answer — if there was one to hire. Or send for a taxi. He must get back into the city. He heard sounds and pushed his way quickly in among some bushes. He crouched low and waited until he heard footsteps and heavy breathing.

Rudi and Elisabeth, who had run all the way, stopped when the village came into view.

'No sign,' Rudi said. 'He may not have come this way. He didn't have much of a start.'

'Probably took another path. If so we'll find him,' Elisabeth replied.

'I'll just stroll into the village and look around. Stay here, Liz.'

'All right.'

The crouching Charles held his breath. He tried to peer through leaves and branches, but he could not see her. There was nothing to do but wait. It seemed a very long time but eventually he heard Rudi's footsteps and then his voice.

'There's no sign of him. Of course I couldn't ask questions. I didn't want to draw attention to myself. He may have turned the wrong way on the mountain road and gone away from Rindt, or else he took one of the woodland paths when he left the cottage. When we get back to the cottage you go in and I'll go on towards Stephanschlag. I shouldn't think he'd go the whole way over the mountains.'

'No, he's much more likely to turn back,' Elisabeth agreed.

'In which case he'll have to pass me. I

wonder why he suddenly decided to run away, just like that.'

'Perhaps because of the shotgun,' Elisabeth suggested. 'It was a bit pointed, wasn't it?'

'I suppose so, but the whole situation was ridiculous. He was staying because he wanted to, not because we were detaining him. I have a feeling there was something else. You didn't have a row with him while I was out getting the paper, did you?'

'Why should I have a row with him,' Elisabeth demanded querulously. 'He's practically a stranger.'

'I don't know. I just wondered. Oh well, come on.'

Charles gave them three or four minutes before emerging from his hiding place among the bushes, and then he strolled to the village. He had no preconceived plan of action. He had merely wanted to get away from the cottage. Now he began to reflect on what would happen if he turned up at his hotel in Borgrad. It would cause quite a stir. He went into the village post office and general store and bought a pair of sunglasses, noticed some shapeless tweed hats and bought one of those too. Then he asked about transport to Borgrad.

'There's a taxi. I'll call him on the telephone if you like.'

'That would be kind of you.'

'You're on holiday here?'

'Er . . . yes. Visiting some friends, but I find they've gone away. Then my car broke down. I can come back for it later, but I must get to Borgrad to attend to some business.'

'I see. Who were your friends?'

Charles pretended not to hear and busied himself inspecting some coloured postcards. The shopkeeper made the phone call and told him that the taxi would be at the door in a matter of moments. When it arrived Charles thanked the man and got into the rather venerable vehicle and gave directions. He sat back moodily.

He was a fool of course, an

irresponsible fool, and he couldn't think what had got into him. He should have escaped the first night and put an end to the whole stupid farce. He certainly did not wish Elisabeth and Rudolf Renner any harm, but it had been ridiculous of him to co-operate in the matter of his own captivity, to take an interest in them to become involved with the silly girl. Now everybody was in an uproar and there was no saying where it would all end. All he wanted to do was to get on a plane and go back to London and forget all about it — but it wouldn't be that simple.

The taxi driver dropped him at the big ornamental fountain in the middle of town, and Charles paid him off. The streets were quiet and he went off in search of a café. He found one in a side street not far from his hotel, bought a Sunday paper and ordered coffee. He read the news again and asked for a second cup.

'It's unusually quiet this morning,' he said to the waiter.

'Yes sir. There's a demonstration. I think people have gone to watch.'

'What are they demonstrating about?' Charles asked.

'This kidnapping,' the man replied, gesturing towards the newspaper on the table top. 'The students say that the Government should cancel the American arms agreement. The time limit expires tomorrow night, you know.'

'So I read. Perhaps I'll go and have a look at the demonstration.'

'You're on holiday here?'

'Yes.'

'German?'

'No, English.'

'One would not have known. The demonstration is outside the Prime Minister's office. Turn left as you go out, walk to the Kaiserhof, turn left there and anyone will tell you where it is.'

'Thank you very much.'

Charles paid for his coffee and went out into the street. He knew very well where the Prime Minister's offices were, in the big Assembly building.

Nobody paid any attention to him as he strolled along. There was no earthly reason why they should. When he turned into the Kaiserstrasse, just beyond the Kaiserhof Hotel, he saw the crowd ahead. It was a larger demonstration than he had expected. There were a number of placards and he was soon able to read some of them. They all said the same thing — scrap the defence agreement. Charles got as close as he could, and then stood with his back to the wall of a building across the road from the Assembly building, and waited and watched.

The crowd were well behaved. There was not a great deal of noise, and no rowdiness. The hard core were obviously students but there were considerable numbers of older people. Charles chatted to a man standing near him, and heard that the demonstration had been going on for about half an hour, that someone had handed in a letter for the Prime Minister, since when nothing had happened.

'It's a shame,' the man said.

'What is?' Charles asked.

'Well, a lot of people don't agree that we should have atomic bases in Carmania. The Government should never have made the agreement. Now some innocent foreigner has been kidnapped and they're going to kill him after tomorrow night.'

'Oh yes. That's too bad, Who are they anyway? Terrorists?'

'No,' the man said scornfully. 'There aren't any terrorists in Carmania. Just some people who don't see eye to eye with the Government, I expect.' Charles concealed a smile. 'The Prime Minister will have to give in.'

'Do you believe that?' Charles asked.

'Yes I do. It's ridiculous. The father of the man they've kidnapped has sent a cable to the United Nations. Carmania has never been involved in any trouble before. Better to stop the American agreement and save the Englishman's life.'

'I wonder how many people think that.'

'Everybody here. Ask them. Hundreds of them — and there are thousands more all over the country, believe me. The Government have made a mistake, and now they'll have to put it right.'

'I see. Interesting.'

It was interesting too. He had had no idea that so many people felt so strongly about the missile bases. Perhaps Elisabeth was correct when she said that the Representatives had voted against the wishes of the people. Perhaps there really was enough feeling in the country to sway the Government, given a little more time.

He waited for a time, but nothing happened. The people were very patient, he thought. The police on duty were mixing with the crowd in a friendly manner, making jokes, chatting to people. He turned and drifted off, still deep in thought. In a few moments he realised that he was across the road from his hotel. He paused irresolutely, and at that moment he saw his father and Janice Innescourt come through the revolving glass doors. His father looked spruce and alert as he always did, and Janice, was beautiful, of course, in her remote rather chilly way. They got into a waiting car and drove off. With a grin Charles wondered what his father thought of Janice's arrival and her surprising news.

Suddenly he made up his mind. It was a pity to call it all off now, just when it seemed that it might succeed. He hailed a taxi coming towards him. 'I'd like to go to Rindt,' he said briskly when he had climbed in.

At Rindt he paid off the driver in the middle of the village and set off along the narrow mountain road. Before long he left it and walked towards the cottage, whistling. He pushed open the door and looked around.

'Hoy,' he called. 'Anyone at home?'

'Charles? Is that you?' He heard

Elisabeth's voice and then she came running from the bedroom. 'You've come back. We thought . . . '

'That I'd escaped. I did. I've been to Borgrad. Where's Rudi?'

'He's gone to Borgrad to confer with the others about what to do. He'll be back soon.'

'Good. Let's have some coffee, shall we?'

'Why did you come back?' she demanded.

'I was enjoying my holiday here,' he answered blandly. 'Did you miss me?'

'What a funny question.' She went into the kitchen and he sauntered after her. He leaned against the door jamb, hands in pockets.

'I meant to buy a couple of shirts while I was out, but I forgot that today's Sunday and the shops were shut in Borgrad.'

'What are you doing with that funny hat?'

'I got that and the sunglasses in the village — a sort of disguise. I didn't want to be recognised.'

'I don't see why not. If you escaped, why did you disguise yourself?'

'There's going to be a terrible commotion when I turn up. I didn't want to be spotted till I was ready.'

'I suppose it all makes sense,' she smiled. 'I don't understand you.'

'I hardly understand myself.'

'Rudi told me that you aren't engaged to that girl, but she says you are.'

'I know. She wants me to marry her. You thought I'd lied to you, didn't you?'

'Yes I did. I was . . . annoyed. I heard about her on the late news broadcast last night and I could hardly sleep I was so cross with you for lying.'

'It was a terrible punishment. That breakfast — ugh. All that cold grease on the plate and the eggs looked like rubber.'

'It was awful, wasn't it?' she laughed.

'I thought so anyway. Now when Rudi comes back we have some talking to do. I've just been watching a demonstration in the city.'

'Tell me about it.'

They carried the coffee out to the garden and he started to tell her.

★   ★   ★

Bruno Jung was in a bad temper. He did not enjoy interference at the best of times. Now he had the press, radio and television breathing heavily down his neck, hundreds of people milling about in the street outside the Assembly building waiting for an answer to their ridiculous letter demanding that he abrogate the agreement immediately, and there was a very curt cable from Grand Duke Philip III, the ruler of Carmania. The Carmanian monarchy might technically be constitutional, but even so Philip had a lot of power and influence and it was not wise to ignore his wishes. The cable read very simply, 'Cancel the agreement. Returning Borgrad shortly'.

So now there would soon be someone else badgering him, and he had not the slightest intention of cancelling the agreement. It was unnecessary. No doubt there would be a similar attempt at interference by the United Nations — they loved to meddle in other people's affairs. Nigel Gresham had started it all. Well, there would be no nickel alloy factory in Carmania just yet. He would not do business with Belmont Industries after this. He wouldn't do anything which might be regarded as an act of hostility towards the company, he would simply insert a few extra conditions which would make the proposed deal less attractive to Belmont. It was an easy enough matter.

He opened a cupboard, took out some excellent brandy, poured a little into a glass, and sipped it. The telephone rang. It was the editor of the newspaper.

'What are you doing about the demonstration outside your office?' the editor demanded.

'Nothing specific. I have received their letter and taken note of it. Someone is out there now, asking them to go home.'

'You don't think they'll accept that for an answer do you?'

'Eventually they'll get tired and go home. It is quite a peaceful crowd.'

'Look here, Dr. Jung, you can't be so high-handed.'

'My dear fellow there are many factors to consider, not the least being the American Government with whom we now have an agreement. I can't enter into a public discussion.'

'Time is running out. You want to be careful your time doesn't run out too. New elections next year, don't forget.'

'Don't you threaten me,' Dr. Jung replied wearily. 'The job isn't worth the money. I'll be quite happy to go back to being a dentist.'

'That's all very well, but what about Charles Gresham?'

'Is this an interview?' the Prime Minister asked testily.

'We can make it one.'

'In that case every effort is being made to ensure Mr. Gresham's safety.'

'My God, I can't print anything as fatuous as that.'

'If you'll wait till later this afternoon I'll have a news conference and make a statement.'

'Then frankly, Prime Minister, I hope it is going to be more co-operative than your attitude so far suggests. To the best of my knowledge there is a great deal of feeling against the agreement in the country, and this kidnapping has brought it to a head. You know what people are like. Under normal circumstances they are willing to be led like sheep, up to a point anyway, rather than go to all the bother of making a fuss. Yet when something like this kidnapping happens, they forget their natural disinclination to do anything. They start to react in a very positive way. It isn't just a question of who is to be Prime Minister after the next elections. That's not very important, when you stop to consider it. Politicians are like princes and come and go, but Carmania goes on. This is a question of our national honour.'

'Why is it,' the Prime Minister asked testily, 'that people have begun to assume that I have no interest in the national honour? There are a great many aspects to this attempt to blackmail the Government, and I have to consider all of them, not just the emotional appeals. Four o'clock here, news conference. Until then I'd rather not discuss matters and I'd be glad if you'd treat this entire conversation as off the record. I've no desire to be quoted out of context.'

'You don't seem very keen to make friends either,' the editor snapped and hung up.

Bruno sighed again and poured a little more brandy. He reconsidered the important points again. The Americans were eager to stick to the agreement. Of course they had not suggested that a kidnapped Englishman be sacrificed on the altar of the arms race. They were much too diplomatic. They had contrived to make it plain that they considered any semi-efficient Prime Minister could handle the situation in such a way that the agreement would stand *and* the Englishman would not be sacrificed. In other words it was up to him to do something about the kidnapping and so save the agreement. Nothing was said about failure, but Bruno Jung was a realist. If he let the Americans down, they wouldn't be so inclined to do him favours in future, and right now — thanks to the oil — the Carmanian economy was closely linked with American enterprise; and there had been talks, interesting talks, about other developments. So there was pressure.

The police and the army had found no trace of the missing man, and this was not surprising, because now the Prime Minister was even more convinced than before that it was the work of amateurs. It was so simple to keep track of known criminals or agitators, but almost impossible to do anything quickly about amateurs. However the fact that they were amateurs had one strong compensatory aspect — they were unlikely to do the Englishman any harm. Real hard-hearted terrorists would have gone about this differently. Bruno Jung had a shrewd suspicion that the kidnappers would be greatly embarrassed if the deadline came and went without any sign of his weakening over the agreement. Heinrich Braun agreed with him on this.

These were the two important points — the steady unobtrusive pressure from Washington, and the fact that he did not believe the wretched man Gresham was in danger. Against them he had to balance the rapidly growing opposition to the agreement. This was something unprecedented. In the past the people of Carmania had indeed displayed the more attractive attributes of sheep. It was difficult to ignore all the letters which were pouring into his office, as well as the offices of the newspaper and the broadcasting station. People were becoming ridiculously agitated. Now the street was blocked by polite but stubborn demonstrators. He glanced out of the window and confirmed his worst suspicions — they showed no signs of dispersing.

He was genuinely unconcerned about next year's elections, although it was not quite true to say that he'd rather go back to being a dentist. His main concern was to do his job well during his term of office and let the future take care of itself. If he gave in to mass demonstrations it would weaken the position not only of his own but of all future governments. If he did not give in, he might precipitate a political crisis with serious consequences.

One more small brandy, and he put away the bottle. The answer was obvious to him. Wait. The crowds would disperse, feelings would subside, Gresham would turn up safe and sound, the agreement would go ahead quietly, and a week or two from now all this would be forgotten. The unpleasant bit was living through the next few days. The intercom on his desk was buzzing and a voice told him that Police Chief Braun was waiting.

'Send him in.'

Braun was looking warm and flustered, and his magnificent uniform, second only to General Schmidt's, was rather sad and crumpled.

'Well?' Jung asked.

'Six more reports. That makes eighteen reports that Charles Gresham has been seen, ten in Borgrad and eight in other parts of the country. All false alarms. Nobody has seen him. Do you know what happened just now?'

'No,' Jung asked, interested. He was always intensely interested in other people's jobs. 'What?'

'A man in the crowd accosted me. Said Gresham was outside, mingling with the crowd, half an hour ago. He actually spoke to him.' Braun snorted.

'Then why didn't he say something

to the nearest policeman?'

'Precisely what I asked him. Do you know what he said? He said that he didn't recognise him till after he'd gone away, because he was wearing dark glasses and a hat with the brim turned down. I tell you, everybody is recognising Gresham, but this is the craziest story of all — as if Gresham would stand around talking to demonstrators if he's managed to get away from his kidnappers. Of course I've had to send someone to telephone the hotel to see if Gresham has shown up, just in case. You have to take every lunatic seriously. No wonder we can't find the wretched man, we waste so much time. Standing outside your office, in the street, talking to a demonstrator! I ask you,' he flung up his arms, 'have you heard anything so ridiculous?'

The Prime Minister smiled and shook his head.

7

'He's right,' Rudi said, nodding his head. 'I saw it myself. There were hundreds of people blocking the street. All of them want the arms deal scrapped.'

'Do you really think they'll give in?' Elisabeth asked doubtfully.

'There's a good chance if you hang on long enough,' Charles replied. 'What's more, I don't think the Government will dare to do anything to you. You'll be popular heroes with a lot of people.'

'They'll have to do something,' Elisabeth retorted, 'but certainly things are improving by the sound of it. We'll see what happens tonight. It's such a pity we haven't got television up here, but reception is hopeless in this area.'

'It was good of you to come back, Charles,' Rudi said gratefully. 'I'm sorry about the shotgun.'

'Forget it. I was in a bad mood, that's all. I decided in Borgrad that we simply can't quit now, not when success may be just around the corner. We must hang on.'

'You're one of us now,' Elisabeth chuckled.

'I think I always have been,' Charles smiled back at her. 'I haven't had so much fun for years. Do you know, I haven't given a single thought to business for two days? This is as good as a rest cure. I would like to write to my father, though. Could I do that? Could someone have it delivered?'

'You write it and I'll have it taken to his hotel,' Rudi promised.

'Good. He'll be worried. I'll make sure he doesn't tell anyone I've written. We don't want to drop any clues accidentally.'

Elisabeth got a writing pad and an envelope for him, and he sat down and began to scribble.

Dear Boss,

I am managing to get this delivered to you, just to let you know that I am well and fighting fit, and in good spirits. Don't please tell anyone I've been in touch with you. I can't explain now, but I shall later. Above all, don't worry.

I'm not engaged to Janice, and after this little episode am not likely to see very much of her in the future. It is a try on. You can assure Mama on that point, as I don't think she likes Janice very much. The poor girl is desperate, so don't blame her too much.

I'll be resigning when I come back. I've been thinking — plenty of time to think, for a change — and I don't want to waste my life in pursuit of money I don't need, and don't want to want . . . if you can follow that.

Please destroy this.

Love,

'Cobweb'.

He sealed the envelope and addressed it. The use of 'Boss', which had been his own personal nickname for his father for years, and signing it 'Cobweb', a hangover from childhood which was unknown outside the family, would assure his father that the letter had not been written under duress. Charles handed it to Rudi.

'There you are. That will cheer up my male parent enormously, and he won't go rushing to the police with it.'

'I'll take the car into town now and see what the latest news is,' Rudi said brightly. 'Be back soon. I'll have lunch there, Liz.'

When he had gone Elisabeth went and stood by the window.

'Is something wrong?' Charles asked.

'No.' She did not turn. 'No, nothing's wrong. I was wondering about you, why you do the things you have done.'

'Why does anyone do anything?' Charles asked humorously.

'I know, but you're doing things out of character. I've begun to realise two things. One is that you've been so very kind to us. You could have got us into a lot of trouble by now. The other is that it's a good job we didn't succeed in kidnapping Jason McCudden. I don't think he'd have behaved like you.'

'I'm quite sure he wouldn't,' Charles agreed. 'Then again, if you'd asked me a week ago, I'd have bet I'd have behaved exactly like Jason McCudden. So why talk about it? I'm on your side now.'

'You always have been.'

'Perhaps.'

'That girl . . . ' Elisabeth began.

There was a pause. 'Janice?' he asked after several seconds.

'Yes. Why should she do a thing like that? Say you were engaged when you aren't? I don't understand.'

'You don't know her. I'm not certain that it's easy to explain.'

'What will you do now?'

'Oh I'll let her down gently. The engagement won't be mentioned again, you'll see. Poor Janice. I'm so sorry for her.'

'Sorry for her? Why?'

'She's spoiled. Her father and mother would do anything for her, and she's got social position and really terribly good looks. She's a wonderful horsewoman — wins prizes and things like that. She plays a decent game of tennis, even better bridge, drive a sports car as well as a man . . . it's tragic.'

'I'm afraid you've lost me. What's tragic about it?'

'Nobody really likes her. She can't help it. She talks down to everybody. She's a snob — and she's so bad that even the other snobs notice it,' he added with a laugh. 'You've never met her so probably you can't understand. She's known all sorts of men ever since she was a schoolgirl — with her social position and looks that was inevitable — but after a few weeks, a few months perhaps, they stop seeing her. She can be very embarrassing, the way she talks to people in shops, for example. She's got a pretty awful voice. I felt desperately sorry for her when I met her, and in a way she's really likeable because she doesn't mean any of it, really wants to be friends and can't understand why nobody else feels the same. That's why I became fairly friendly with her.'

'I see — or I think I do.'

'After this little episode, however, I shan't be seeing very much of her. She had no right to do what she did. She's assuming that I'll be too gentlemanly to contradict her, and that I'll buy a ring and in due course trot meekly along to church in a grey topper and marry her. It won't work.'

'Perhaps I feel sorry for her too,' Elisabeth said slowly. 'Is she in love with you?' She turned to face him as she asked the question. He looked at her directly.

'I don't know. I honestly don't know. Maybe she is, maybe not. She is probably influenced by several things

— fear of remaining unmarried; probably pressure from her parents; money I think, because I suspect death duties are going to hit her pretty hard unless she's prepared to sell their house and land; and perhaps, in her own way, love. Who can say?'

'Your life has been turned upside down in three days, hasn't it?'

He laughed. 'It has. I've been kidnapped, I'm having a lovely holiday, I'm conspiring to have a defence agreement torn up, I've become engaged behind my back . . . oh, lots of things have happened. It does one good to be shaken up occasionally. I was living in a rut — pleasant perhaps, but a rut. I told my father . . . well, I told him I'm resigning my job.'

'Why did you do that?' she demanded incredulously.

'Because of you. You were the one who made me realise that I'm devoting my time to earning money I can't spend. You showed me that there is a better life.'

'I did? I don't see how you reach that conclusion. I was interested in all you told me, and it seemed funny that I owned my own car and you didn't; but I didn't tell you that mine is a better life.'

'No, but it is. You've got something to look forward to. I haven't. I've got it all already. I've had enough.'

'What will you do?'

'I shall buy myself a house in the north of Herefordshire, around Pembridge, I think. My father was born in Pembridge. I think I'll open a little business, just to give myself an interest in life. An antique shop perhaps, or local handicrafts, something like that. I've got to have something to do, after all.'

'Suppose the business succeeds and you end up owning a chain of shops?'

'Nobody does that in Herefordshire. They're much too sensible. At any rate I shan't. Probably I'll lose money.'

'Are you serious, Charles?'

He stared at her as though looking at a stranger, and indeed he had a weird feeling that he was seeing her for the first time.

'I am serious. Now you can see what you started when you decided to kidnap Jason McCudden. The Americans may lose a missile base, McCudden may get into trouble with the President, Bruno Jung could lose the next election, Belmont Industries has just lost its chairman — and of course you and your brother may end up in the salt mines. Serve you right,' he added with a grin.

'You make it sound so terrible.'

'Let's see if there's any news. Did you say I could have lunch?'

'I'm sorry. Of course. I'll go and make it now.'

'Can't I help?'

'If you wish.'

They took the transistor into the kitchen and he peeled a few potatoes while she did other things. As usual, the kidnapping still held pride of place in the news. Now, however, a new tone had crept in. The Prime Minister was obviously under attack and the television people gave a lot of prominence to the outcry in various parts of the country. There had been meetings in different towns and petitions were flooding in to Government offices.

'I wonder if Jung can hold out,' Charles said when it was over. 'It isn't going to be easy for him. The TV people are not on his side. You can tell by the way they present the news.'

'Poor Prime Minister,' Elisabeth murmured, 'and he was quite a good dentist too. Ready with the potatoes?' she added.

'Yes, here you are.'

He stood back and watched her at work, her head bent so that her soft dark hair obscured her features. She was graceful he thought. Not many women could contrive to be attractive bent over a stove. At least he didn't think so.

'Why have you never married?' he asked abruptly.

'You asked me that before.' She did

161

not look up as she spoke.

'Did I? What's the answer?'

'There's plenty of time and I've never met anyone I really want to marry.'

'Doesn't anyone want to marry you?'

'There is someone, yes, but he's never asked me. If he does, the answer is no.'

'Hard hearted, aren't you? It's a pity. You'd make a success of being married. You'd have a talent for it.'

'You sound like an expert. Are you?'

'Not guilty. I just think you could make yourself and someone else very happy if you married.'

'A better wife than a kidnapper, is that it?' she asked, closing the oven door.

'I don't know,' he replied diffidently, 'I rather like you as a kidnapper.'

'You're a special sort of victim, though, aren't you?' she pointed out, turning. 'Come along. We can leave this for a bit. Can you play draughts?'

'I did once, years and years ago.'

'Then you can give me a game now while we're waiting for lunch.'

* * *

The letter from Charles to his father was delayed for almost twenty-four hours. Rudi did not want to go to Nigel's hotel himself and he made arrangements for a friend to slip the letter onto the reception desk. His friend, however, fell downstairs and knocked himself out, was taken to hospital suffering from concussion and not discharged until the next day, just before lunch.

So while Charles and Elisabeth dallied happily in the woods for another glorious day, tension mounted everywhere and Nigel's confidence ebbed alarmingly.

On Monday afternoon the letter arrived. Nigel Gresham answered the door of his hotel room and found a bell boy with a salver.

'Letter for you, sir.'

He picked it up. Handwritten, no stamp . . . then his heart thumped. He knew that handwriting well.

'Where did you get this?'

'The receptionist told me to bring it up, sir.'

'Thank you.' He tipped the boy and closed the door. He slit open the letter and read it. Then he read it again.

So all was well, was it? What exactly did that mean? If Charles had been forced to write the letter he would never have used nicknames, so that meant the letter was voluntary and genuine. It was a mystery. What was he up to? *Had* he been kidnapped? That was a sobering question.

Nigel picked up the telephone and booked a call to London. After that he spoke to the hotel receptionist and asked who had delivered the letter.

'I didn't see him sir. I was busy at the time. Someone walked in and left an envelope on the desk. I picked it up a few moments later and saw it was for you, so I sent it up. The man had gone. I didn't get a good look at him.'

'It was a man?'

'Oh yes — at least I think so. I had no

reason to notice the person, sir. Is something wrong?'

'No, not at all. I was just curious to know who had brought the letter. I thought it might have been a friend. Thank you.'

Not very helpful, he thought. One thing was fairly obvious. Jung wasn't going to let himself be stampeded into anything. The agreement was not going to be broken yet. It was a relief, therefore, to see the jaunty tone of the letter. He re-read the bit about Janice. Damn the girl's eyes, he thought huffily. What a disreputable thing to do. And he couldn't say a thing about it . . . yet.

His call came through quickly and he heard his wife's voice on the line.

'Hullo darling, that was fast work. How are you?'

'All right, Nigel. What news of Charles?'

'Strictly between ourselves he's managed to get a letter to me secretly, and he's asked me not to tell the police so you mustn't talk about it to anyone. He says he's fine and that we are not to worry.'

'Perhaps they made him write it.'

'I wondered, but he called me 'Dear Boss' and signed himself 'Cobweb'. I think that means he really is all right. Nobody's called him Cobweb for years, and he's the only person to call me Boss as though it were my name. Yes, I think we can take heart.'

'Are they cancelling the agreement?'

'Nothing official, but I don't think so.'

'Then what will happen?'

'We must wait and see, my dear. At least we have Charles's letter. I called you at once. Oh, and some more good news.'

'What's that?'

'He is *not*, repeat *not*, engaged to Janice. It seems she made the announcement all by herself, to force his hand. He isn't going to marry her.'

'That's a bit awkward. I've had calls from her parents about the engagement. They're full of it.'

'They would be. Well they're all wrong. I tell you what, you pack a bag and hop on a plane and come here. Ring Sanderson and tell him to fix it all, and telephone me with flight details. If he's not at the office they'll know where you can get hold of him.'

'It would be nice to get away. Lady Innescourt said she is coming up to Town tomorrow.'

'All the more reason to avoid her. We must keep out of the way until Charles has sorted out the mess. Let me think. I've got the wretched girl here, staying on the same floor of the hotel if you please. I know, I'll telephone the British Ambassador and ask him to put us up.'

'The Ambassador? Do you know him?'

'Not very well. He's Hugh Maddox.'

'Diana's husband?'

'That's right. I've been meaning to call him anyway but I haven't had time.'

'I thought they were in South America.'

'They're not. They're here and he's

an Ambassador now. He should be able to put us up all right. I'll call when we've finished talking. It will be interesting to meet him again after all these years of exchanging Christmas cards and your writing to his wife.'

'She used to be my best friend.'

'Let's hope the friendship extends to an invitation. I'll meet you at the airport. Make sure Sanderson telephones me as soon as he has confirmed all the details.'

He hung up shortly afterwards, and then telephoned a startled British Ambassador and said he wanted to come and stay with him for several days. Hugh Maddox was cordial and said he'd send an Embassy car in an hour.

His arrangements made, Nigel packed his suitcase quickly and sent for a porter to take it down to reception. He went down and paid his bill, rather to the hotel's regret because they were sorry to lose such a lucrative customer, and went into the lounge to wait.

He had said nothing to his wife about

Charles's threat to resign from the group. It was something they could talk about later at their leisure, but meantime it caused him to think hard. What had been happening to Charles? There was something going on that nobody knew about, something very mysterious indeed. He was supposed to be in durance vile, literally on the eve of his execution, and yet he wrote a cheerful letter and said he was retiring from the company.

Nigel gave up after a quarter of an hour. There were obviously things he didn't know, material evidence without which he couldn't possibly hope to appreciate what was going on. All he could do now was to wait. His call from London came through just before he left the hotel, and he jotted down his wife's flight number and time. Then the Embassy car arrived and he had his suitcase carried out.

When Janice tried to telephone him an hour later she was shaken to be told that he had booked out and left no forwarding address other than his London one. Afternoon drew into evening. The main news broadcast of the day in Borgrad was at seven o'clock, both on radio and television. That evening, as seven o'clock approached, people all over the country glanced at their watches and switched on. There would be a statement of some sort now. There had to be. This was the last evening.

At the cottage up in the mountains Rudi, Elisabeth and Charles sat together waiting. In the British Embassy the Ambassador, his wife and his guests sat staring at the television screen. Other Embassy staff were doing the same. In his house, Bruno Jung put away some papers and switched on his television. Heinrich Braun was checking that his police patrols were all up to strength and that his instructions had been followed, in case there were any sort of demonstration. Hans Grotben, Dirk Gerlach, Walther Gruneberg and Willi Fischer were on edge; waiting to see if Elisabeth's scheme had worked.

They had all been kept pretty much in the dark these past few days and were anxious to know if she had pulled it off after all.

Then the announcers told the waiting world.

'In an interview earlier this afternoon, the Prime Minister, Dr. Bruno Jung, told reporters that the Government of Carmania would not yield to blackmail by the terrorists who kidnapped the British businessman, Mr. Charles Gresham, three days ago.

' 'We have entered into a solemn agreement with the United States Government,' Dr. Jung said. 'Carmania will not go back on its word because of the criminal actions of irresponsible people who disagree with the constitutional processes of democratic government. We call upon the kidnappers to release the innocent man whom they are holding in captivity. They will not achieve their purposes by such methods. The Government will never give way to such threats.' Dr. Jung also asked people to consider what sort of peace of mind or security Carmania would know in the future once it permitted itself to be dictated to in matters of national or international policy.

'Asked about Mr. Gresham's safety, Dr. Jung said that every effort was still being made to trace the missing Englishman and that all the country's resources were bent towards that end. He was still hopeful that a release would be effected before the deadline.

'Mr. Nigel Gresham, father of the missing man, was not available for interview. A little earlier this evening he moved out of his hotel in Borgrad and is now staying with Mr. Hugh Maddox, the British Ambassador.

'Miss Janice Innescourt, fiancée of the missing man, said that Prime Minister Jung's attitude was inhuman and intolerable. She appealed to the kidnappers to release Mr. Gresham who, she said, had done them no harm and was not in any way involved in negotiations between the American Government and Carmania.

'Grand Duke Philip, who has cut short his visit to Baratavia where he recently became engaged to Her Royal Highness Princess Fiona-Alina, is expected to arrive at the airport later this evening. There are unconfirmed reports that he has asked the Prime Minister to terminate the defence agreement and so save Mr. Gresham's life.'

The country was almost evenly divided into two schools of thought: those who agreed that it would be fatal to allow terrorists to dictate to the Government, and those who thought that human life was infinitely more important than political pieces of paper. Most disappointed of all, however, were the conspirators. Elisabeth took it especially to heart.

'You don't want to worry,' Charles told her, putting an arm around her shoulders. 'Hang on for a bit and let public opinion do your work for you. You've only lost a battle, not a war, as somebody said once. In fact, even that is overstating it. They haven't given in by the deadline you set, but that doesn't mean that they won't later on.'

'No.' She shook her head and averted her face. 'It was a gamble which hasn't come off. They've decided to call our bluff. They won't change their minds, Charles. Not now. Tomorrow we'll take you back to Borgrad and we'll go home. It's all over.'

'Rubbish. You will not take me back to Borgrad. We'll go for a nice walk in the woods together.'

'No. What will you say, Charles?'

'I'll say I was blindfolded, don't know where I was taken, and that my captors were always masked. Hang it, Elisabeth, don't be so gloomy. Wait for a day or two. There's plenty of time.'

She shook her head again. 'It's no use, I tell you. We've failed. Rudi?'

'You're right, Liz,' he agreed wearily. 'It was worth the try. Don't take it to heart. If you'd only seen that last demonstration. A lot of people were on our side. Now we'll have our atomic bases and that's the end of it. Maybe it will all work out in the long run.'

'Why don't we play cards?' she suggested.

Charles and Rudi exchanged glances. 'All right,' they agreed.

They settled down to a gloomy evening.

8

Charles awoke and glanced at his watch. Midnight! He rolled over and tried to get back to sleep but it was impossible. He tossed and turned till a quarter to one and at last got up and turned on the light. He had gone to bed early, at half past ten, but he had only slept fitfully. He slipped on some clothes and went into the kitchen to make some hot chocolate. As he busied himself at his task he realised with sudden clarity that he would miss the cottage. He really had enjoyed himself here. It was a pity it hadn't lasted a little longer.

He took his drink outside and sat on the top step in the moonlight, sipping the scalding chocolate. He heard a noise and turned. Elisabeth, in a light coloured dressing gown, stood in the doorway.

'Hullo. Where's Rudi?' he asked.

'Gone to bed. There's no real point in one of us staying awake all night, is there?'

'No, of course not. I couldn't sleep.'

'Neither could I,' she said. 'What are you drinking?'

'Chocolate. Shall I get you some?'

'No thanks,' she said. 'I'm not thirsty. I'll just sit beside you.'

She came over and sat down close to him, and pushed her hair out of her eyes. He smiled at her, but the smile she gave in reply was a half-hearted affair.

'I can imagine how you're feeling tonight,' he said gently, 'but honestly you mustn't lose heart so quickly. Be patient.'

'It's not that,' she contradicted. 'I was just restless. The other thing doesn't really matter. We've tried and we've failed. Perhaps we weren't meant to succeed. Perhaps my point of view isn't so right after all. Who am I to try to coerce a government?'

'A person,' he replied mildly. 'A

citizen. I must admit I'm glad you're not brooding too much on the subject. If you could just detach your feelings a little and stand back and be more objective, you wouldn't take it all so personally.' He laughed. 'Listen to who is talking! I haven't allowed myself to become personally involved in anything for years.'

'What was keeping you awake?' Elisabeth asked.

'That's a good question. As a matter of fact I lay thinking of how much I'd like to stay on here for a little longer. I'm not in any hurry to pick up the threads of my life. I hope Rudi and you will give it at least another week. I think a lot could happen in that time.'

'You're quite an optimist,' she remarked, putting her chin on her hands. 'I've got two weeks' holiday from work. I wonder what I shall do for the rest of it?'

'You've used up part of your holiday for this? I suppose you had to. What about Rudi?'

'He took a week's leave. Originally, you see, we were all going to take it in turns. There would have been three shifts of two, plus me here all the time to do the cooking and washing. All that changed when Rudi and I decided to look after you ourselves. It was safer for the others. Rudi told them in the factory that he was taking a week off.'

'Why don't you go away? Go to Salzburg for a few days and relax.'

'No money,' she answered dryly. 'We're both a bit broke this summer. Probably we'll get out the tents and go off camping for a few days. We used to like camping when we were children.'

'Sounds great. I wish I were coming.'

'What will you do anyway?'

'Talk to my father about business, and then I expect I'll have to go directly to the United States. No more lotus eating, not for a little while.'

'You said you had resigned.'

'I know, but I've one or two loose ends to tie up which I can't just walk off and leave. It will take about three weeks, then I can go back to England, sell Tabarie, and look for another house. That ought to keep me occupied for a time. No more walks in the woods for me, not for a long while — and then I'll be walking alone.'

'I'm sure you needn't if you don't want to — be alone, I mean. I think I'll try to get to sleep again. Good night, Charles.'

'Hang on.' He scrambled to his feet and took her hand. 'Must you go?'

'It's late. We can't sit here all night.'

'I don't see why not. We can do as we please,' he answered with a grin.

'You know, I believe you really are having a holiday,' she laughed.

'Thanks to you.' He squeezed her hand. 'If it hadn't been for you it would have been different.'

She coloured and tried to free her hands, but he held on to her.

'I mean it, Elisabeth. I don't think I'd have stayed, were it not for you. I'd have escaped somehow.'

'That's ridiculous.' Her eyes refused to meet his.

Slowly he pulled her towards him and kissed her, very gently. She stood like a stone, unresponsive, rigid.

'I'm sorry.' He dropped his hands. Something was wrong, he didn't know what. 'I'm sorry, Elisabeth.'

She turned and fled into the cottage and he sat on the steps again and sighed. Everything seemed to be turning sour again.

Elisabeth, meantime, was leaning against the closed bedroom door. She could see Rudi in the dark, lying fast asleep in his bed. She switched on the table lamp and shook him. He wakened slowly, grumbling.

'I'm tired. What's the time?'

'Half past midnight.'

'What the blazes?' He sat up and blinked at her.

'I couldn't sleep. Rudi, let's get up very early and go home, before Charles is awake.'

'You mean leave him here?'

'Why not? He's got money. He can find his own way back. Let's just get out and forget the whole thing. We can leave before six.'

'I suppose so. What's all the rush, and why not give Charles a lift into the city?'

'I don't want to see him.'

He knitted his brows anxiously, disturbed by her tone.

'Is something wrong, Liz?'

'No!'

'You're not very convincing. Has he been doing anything? If he's been annoying you I'll . . . '

'Don't be so stupid, Rudi. If you must know, I love him and that's why I want to get away from him.'

'Love him?' He gaped at his sister. 'Charles Gresham, a foreigner, who's got more money than you and I put together will ever see in a lifetime? How did this happen?'

'How do I know? It just happened. You don't think I enjoy it, do you?' she asked pathetically.

'Has he been making passes at you?'

'Of course not, Rudi. I don't want to spend another minute with him — it only makes it worse.'

'Oh gosh.' He put an arm round his sister's shoulders. 'I'm sorry Liz I really am. I thought you and Kurt Schwarz . . . well, everybody's expecting you to get married.'

'They'll have to go on expecting. I like Kurt, but not that much.'

'Charles Gresham of all people! Well, if that's the case, then we'll go away and leave him. As you said, he can find his own way back. He won't betray us.'

'No, he won't,' she agreed. 'There's nothing else to link us with the kidnapping, not that I can think of. I believe we'll be safe. I'll come back here next week and clear up before I go back to work. Why don't we go camping for a few days?'

'That's a good idea but I have a better one. Why don't we get a few hours' sleep?'

He kissed her cheek and watched as

she crossed the room to the other bed and snuggled up under the bedclothes. Then he switched out the light and lay for a time, disturbed.

Elisabeth, too, remained awake for quite a long time, and Charles even longer. His emotions were in a turmoil. It was ages since he had kissed a girl. He didn't seem to have had much time for that sort of thing recently. For her to respond like that, with cold, stony aloofness, was shattering. What was worse, she wasn't just any girl, she was beginning to occupy an important place in his thoughts. A long time later he drifted off to sleep. He slept well into the morning and woke up to the sound of birds. The sunlight flooded the room as he rubbed his eyes and reached for his expensive wristwatch. Ten. Ten? Good heavens.

He rushed into the bathroom for a wash and then flung on his clothes. There was nobody in the living room so he tried the kitchen, then the other bedroom. Funny, he thought, very funny. He went outside. No sign of life there either. Almost as an afterthought he looked in the little woodshed in a clearing a few yards away, where the car was garaged. That was empty too.

Puzzled, Charles walked back into the house and switched on the coffee percolator and began to boil some eggs and make toast. The place was deadly quiet. Then he thought of something. He went back to the other bedroom and looked under the beds. No suitcases. Hurriedly he opened and closed all the drawers and searched in the big built-in cupboards. Still nothing. Back to the bathroom to look in the other glass fronted cabinet, the one he didn't use. Again nothing.

He walked back to the kitchen very slowly and sat down to two very hard boiled eggs and some burnt toast. He didn't even notice. Elisabeth and Rudi had gone. They'd taken everything. Why hadn't they woken him to let him know? What was happening. He munched his way through a breakfast which tasted like sawdust and went back into the living room again. There he found it, where it had fallen from the mantelpiece into a corner of the fireplace — an envelope with his name on it.

Eagerly he opened it and sat down to read. Less eagerly he read it again. It was from Elisabeth, a short farewell note. They'd gone home. He was free. They were sorry for all the trouble they had caused and grateful to him for being so understanding and kind about it. Just that, nothing else; written in excellent English. He folded up the letter, put it back into its envelope, and sat down to think. There was much to think about.

★ ★ ★

There was a meeting of the erstwhile Committee for Carmanian Neutrality in the Renners' flat. They sat in the spacious book-lined sitting room and talked moodily.

'How can you be sure this fellow Gresham won't tell the police all about you?' Kurt Schwarz demanded. Kurt had been very much out of things and it had hurt his vanity just a little. 'You say he knows your names and all about you.'

'Yes, it was my fault. I gave the game away,' Elisabeth admitted. 'I think Rudi will agree that he was very friendly. We believe he won't talk.'

'She's right,' Rudi agreed. 'We've nothing to worry about there. We were very lucky over Charles Gresham.'

'So we just drop the whole thing, do we?' asked Willi Fischer, the farmer, rubbing a speck of dirt from the barrel of his shotgun. 'It's all over now?'

'I'm afraid so,' Elisabeth nodded. 'I've been thinking, though, about all those letters to the press, the demonstration, telephone calls, all the things we've been hearing about. We may have lost this particular battle, but they'll think twice before they risk upsetting public opinion again.

Another time they may have a referendum.'

'*If* there's another time,' Kurt grumbled. 'This was the one we wanted to stop, not something in the future that we don't even know about yet. What about that old fool Jung, just sitting back and doing nothing? It would have served him right if we'd killed the Englishman and left him on the steps of the Prime Minister's house.'

'Poor Mr. Gresham,' Elisabeth murmured and the others laughed.

'Well, you know what I mean. They've no idea who did the kidnapping — or I hope they haven't. We could have been deadly serious.'

'You know what will happen, don't you?' Walther Gruneberg asked. 'Belmont Industries will cancel their plans to open a factory in Carmania. Gresham and his father can hardly be expected to feel friendly in view of the fact that Gresham was left to his fate. So we lose a factory and two thousand good jobs, just so that we can have guided missiles pointing at Russia or even China. It's ridiculous.'

'You should write to the papers about it,' Elisabeth suggested. 'After all, we may as well get as much fun out of the situation as we can. Rudi and I are going off for three days, camping. We'll miss this week's music circle. Anyway, it's better if we don't see too much of one another until all the fuss has died down, just in case the police ever get a smell of our trail.'

They all nodded agreement, and after coffee and biscuits they began to leave. Kurt Schwarz lingered on till last, and when Rudi left the room he crossed over to where Elisabeth sat. 'I've been worried about you, Elisabeth. You've no idea how much.'

'Thank you, Kurt.'

'School breaks up next week. Have you got any more holidays to come?'

'Another two weeks,' Elisabeth admitted.

'Perhaps we could have a holiday together?' he suggested boldly.

'I don't think that would be a very

good idea, Kurt. People might think things.'

'Let them think. I don't mind.'

'Perhaps not, but I do.' Her smile took the sting out of her words. 'Anyway I don't want a holiday this summer. I've got another week of my present leave to come, and that will do me till January or February.'

'Well, next week perhaps you would come out to dinner, and we could go to the theatre?'

She shook her head. 'I'm sorry Kurt, but I don't feel like celebrating.'

'You mustn't let this business bother you. It wasn't your fault that Bruno Jung turned out to be a callous monster.'

'It isn't that. I'm not worried about that now. It's all over and I want to forget it.'

'What's wrong then?'

'Nothing. I just feel like my own company.'

'You're a strange girl.' He summoned up his courage. 'I've . . . I've wanted to ask you for a long time. About getting married, I mean. I'd like to marry you, Elisabeth. What do you say?'

She patted his hand and shook her head again. 'Thank you Kurt, but I can't accept. You're a good friend, but I don't feel about you that way. I'm sorry Kurt.'

'Oh. You mean you won't marry me?' He had always expected that when he made up his mind to ask her, she would accept. He would be a head teacher in a few years. As it was he was head of the mathematics department. He had a good salary and owned his own house. It was a very suitable arrangement and he was extremely fond of her. He didn't want to marry anyone else.

'That's what I mean, I'm afraid.'

'Elisabeth, is something wrong? Has something happened?'

'No, Kurt.'

'I always thought . . . '

'I've never said anything to make you believe I was going to marry you, have I?' she asked.

'No, but . . . everybody has always understood . . . you make it difficult for me.'

She was far too honest to play word games with him. 'Kurt we've always been good friends and I know some people expected us to marry. I've guessed for a long time that one day you would ask me. Now that the time has come, the answer must be no. I don't love you, Kurt.'

He fidgeted awkwardly. He did not like talk about love. It was an irrational, romantic state. How like a woman to drag it into a serious conversation about marriage.

'I'm sure that given time we would settle down nicely.'

'Poor Kurt,' she laughed. 'Marriage means a little more to me than that.'

'Is there someone else? I've seen Hans Grotben looking at you. Grotben is quite junior, and he's frivolous in his attitude towards his work. Why . . . '

'It isn't Hans Grotben,' she interrupted patiently. 'Or Walther or Willi or anyone else. You can stop your match-making, Kurt. Right now I'm not thinking about marrying.'

'Oh? Well, when shall I see you again?'

'Next time I attend the Music Circle, I expect. Thank you Kurt, but I'm sorry I just can't accept.'

'There's plenty of time,' he answered philosophically. 'Perhaps you'll change your mind.'

Elisabeth did not disenchant him. Rudi returned to the room, and a few minutes later a disappointed Kurt left.

'I hope I stayed away long enough,' Rudi said, amused. 'I thought Kurt wanted to get you alone.'

'He did. He thinks I'd make a good wife.'

'So he's got round to it, has he?' Rudi chuckled. 'I wondered if he'd ever pluck up courage. You turned him down, of course.'

'Yes. Do you think I was wrong, Rudi?'

'He's too much of a dry stick for you,

Liz. I bet he said it would be an extremely suitable arrangement.'

'Not exactly. He did say, though, that we would settle down nicely in time.'

'How romantic,' Rudi laughed. 'Poor Liz.' He put an arm around her.

'Why poor me?'

'You're in love with the Englishman, and the only person who has proposed is a man who thinks the word love has something to do with mothers and babies, and nothing whatever to do with rational, highly educated school teachers.' He squeezed her shoulders. 'That's why I said poor Liz.'

'I'm a fool over Charles,' she admitted.

'I suppose he's much too important to take people like us seriously. Mind you, he was attracted. I know he was.'

'You're guessing,' she said with a nervous laugh.

'If you mean he didn't say so to me, then I agree I'm guessing, but one doesn't always have to be told things in order to know them. Never mind, there will be someone else one day.'

'Yes,' she agreed meekly. 'No doubt you're right.'

'So let's pack. We've got time to get there tonight if we get a move on.'

'Good.' She got up briskly. 'Let's hurry up.'

They left about an hour later in Rudi's car which was laden with camping equipment. Their destination was a secluded valley in the foothills of the Ewald Mountains, behind the town of Beckburg. There, beside a stream, was a perfect camping ground, with trees all round to act as a windbreak. By seven o'clock they had pitched the tents, unpacked, and Elisabeth was frying their supper over a Primus stove. They turned in early and that night she slept really soundly for the first time for several days. So began three days of rest and reflection.

Sometimes they sat by the stream, sometimes they went walking. There was a hamlet abut a mile away where Rudi drank beer and Elisabeth would order a pot of coffee. There, in the country, the air seemed fresher, the food tasted better, and they slept like children. The memories of the cottage began to fade a little, to blur at the edges. She hadn't got Charles Gresham out of her system — perhaps she never would — but she was adjusting to the situation. It was as though she were wiping the slate clean, ready to start again.

They had brought no radio and they bought no newspapers. The whole idea was to get away from things. Naturally she spent quite a lot of time wondering just what Charles was doing, how he had explained his absence, what he had said about his kidnappers, for of course he had to say *something*. His parents would be delighted to see him safe. Poor Janice Innescourt would be disillusioned by now. Elisabeth felt rather a sisterly affection for Janice. After all, they both wanted Charles Gresham and neither of them could have him. Neither of them was right for a merchant prince, she thought with amusement. Janice was too grand and she, Elisabeth, was undoubtedly much too insignificant. It was a pity he had kissed her like that, because it polarised her feelings and gave them form and substance. To him she would be just a pretty girl he had met, an amusing one who had kidnapped him by mistake, who had cooked his meals and gone walking in the woods with him. Would he remember her a year from now?

Then again, would she remember him — or more precisely, *how* would she remember him? Time changes all things, which was rather sad. When they got back she must buy the back issues of the newspaper and follow the story of his release, and what everyone had said. That at least would be amusing and interesting. She ought to make up a scrapbook of the kidnapping.

Tactfully Rudi did not mention Charles Gresham's name. Instead he spent his idle moments composing a long letter to his current girl friend who was an air hostess. Elisabeth wondered if this time he was serious. Rudi collected girl friends the way some people collect beer mugs or matchbox labels. She did not ask him outright, for she did not like to pry into his affairs. They were private to him, and when he had something to tell her, he would do so. There was a considerable depth of understanding between them.

On the last evening, before they had supper, they walked by the edge of the gurgling stream.

'Everything all right?' Rudi asked, making his first oblique reference to her state of mind.

'Fine, Rudi. I feel like a different person.'

'Good.' He squeezed her hand. 'I'm glad. So do I, but it isn't so important in my case. What will you do with yourself during the second week of your holiday?'

'Laze, read, go to the cinema occasionally. Nothing exciting. Read mainly. I'm going to the library on Monday.'

'While I give the benefit of my genius to Tagrad Electronics. Lucky you. Anyway, I'm glad you're looking better and more cheerful. You had me worried.'

The smiles they exchanged were smiles of close comradeship. That night, just after they had finished supper, it began to rain. They turned in and it poured down all night, one of the regular but infrequent summer rain storms which were a feature of the Carmanian climate. Elisabeth lay snug inside her sleeping bag and listened to the noise and felt safe and contented. Let the elements rage, she was safe from them.

Next morning the storm had passed and they packed up and drove back to the city in bright sunlight. The world had a fresh, clear, polished appearance, as though all its cares had been washed away by the rain storm.

9

Elisabeth and Rudi read the newspapers incredulously. The search for the missing English businessman continued unabated and there was no trace of him. No contact had been made by the kidnappers. A strange silence, considering that their deadline had expired four days previously. All the headlines asked the same question — was Charles Gresham still alive? Or did the kidnappers' silence have another, more sinister connotation? It was a fruitful field for speculation.

There were other stories in the back issues. Grand Duke Philip was greatly distressed by events, apparently, and it was an open secret now that he disagreed profoundly with Dr. Jung on how the affair should have been handled. Jason McCudden had returned from Washington, professionally non-committal when interviewed, but presumably satisfied now that the defence agreement was safe. Nigel and Nancy Gresham were still staying with the British Ambassador, and Janice Innescourt was still at the big four star hotel and still appealing to the kidnappers to return her lover. However there was a photograph of her with a man, Count Johannes von Galland, from Baratavia, who was visiting Carmania partly on business, partly on holiday. Studying the photograph with considerable interest, Elisabeth decided that Janice Innescourt did not look terribly distressed. Perhaps the count made a pleasing diversion. The whereabouts of Charles was a first class mystery.

'Where the devil has he gone?' Rudi asked for the tenth time, throwing up his hands. 'How can he still be missing? Oh well, we'd better drive over to Rindt and see if everything is all right at the cottage. That's the first thing.'

Elisabeth nodded agreement and they drove up to the mountains right away. The cottage was unoccupied.

Everything was neat and tidy, no dirty dishes, beds made, no signs of life. Mystified they drove into the village, bought some sweets in the shop and chatted to the proprietor. They brought up the question of the missing English-man.

'We had the police here two days ago, on Thursday,' the shopkeeper said. 'They searched the whole area, calling at every house.' He looked more closely at Rudi. 'You have the old Forest Supervisor's cottage, don't you?'

'Yes, it's ours.'

'They asked about it. They found it lying empty. I said I thought you used it at weekends. That's right, isn't it?'

Rudi nodded. 'Occasionally,' he confirmed.

'They went round all the empty chalets and cottages,' the shopkeeper went on, 'and asked a tremendous number of questions. We had a man in here one morning buying sunglasses and one of those tweed hats over there, a stranger. They were quite interested in him until I told them he was a German. It seems he's the only stranger we've had around these parts.'

'We met him,' Rudi said blandly. 'A nice chap. Is he still around?'

'It's funny you should ask that, because he was in here yesterday. He said his holiday was over and that he was on his way back to Bonn. I remember wondering where he had been staying. Perhaps he was camping. The funny thing is that the first time he came in he wanted a taxi to take him to Borgrad because his car had broken down. Quite a mystery, but nothing to do with the Englishman.'

'Just so. He's gone, then?'

'Yes, he hired the taxi again, so I wonder what's happened to his own car this time. I've been meaning to ask old Peter what sort of luggage he had. We don't get many strangers up here, as you know.'

'Quite,' Rudi agreed. 'Well, thanks a lot. We must be getting back to town. We just came up to fetch a few things from the cottage.'

They got into the car and drove back slowly, decidedly puzzled. 'What was Charles doing here yesterday?' Rudi asked his sister.

'I can't imagine. I wonder where he is now. He can't leave the country — he'd be picked up by the immigration people at once. The whole thing is inexplicable. I wish I knew what he was up to.'

'It sounds as though he stayed on at the cottage until yesterday, and that's what I can't follow,' Rudi replied. 'Why should he have done that?'

'We'll see what the news is when we get back.'

'Could he have been in an accident?'

'It doesn't seem likely, does it?' she asked.

The questions were fruitless and the answers non-existent, so they lapsed into silence until they reached the city. There they received a surprise. The morning's news concerned Charles all right. According to the radio, a letter had been received by the Police Chief.

It had been dropped on the steps of the Central Police Station where a passer-by found it and handed it in. It was from Charles and begged the police to tell the Prime Minister that his life was now in grave danger and that unless something happened very quickly, he would certainly be killed. The whole affair had boiled up again. There were now foreign press men in the country and everybody was interviewing the Prime Minister, the Police Chief, Charles's parents, the Grand Duke — everyone except Janice Innescourt who, apparently, had nothing to say at the moment.

'What the devil?' Rudi exclaimed when he heard. 'His life in danger? From whom?'

'Can't you see what he's doing?' Elisabeth said. 'He's keeping the thing alive. Don't you remember how he urged us not to give up? Well, when we gave up, he decided to stay in hiding. Naturally everyone assumed that the kidnappers still had him. Now that he's written this note it means he's going it all alone, Rudi. Gosh I bet Kurt and Hans and the others are frantic over this. Probably they've been trying to contact us for days.'

'So *that's* it. Of course. The happy hostage — he just won't go home! Well, what do we do now?'

'You'd better contact the others and tell them to stop worrying. Explain it to them. Meantime I think I'll do some exploring.'

'Exploring?'

'Investigating is a better word. I'm going to interview Nigel Gresham and also Janice Innescourt. I'd like to see what sort of people they are. I am Trudi Haffner from some German magazine. I'll think of one. I wonder if Charles will try to get in touch with us? He doesn't know this address, but he knows where we both work. He could find out that way.'

'Perhaps he wants to keep us out of it,' Rudi suggested. 'We'll see.'

Brother and sister went their separate ways. Elisabeth telephoned the British

Embassy and after much argument was put through to Nigel Gresham. He was awkward but she was persistent and at last, much against his judgement he agreed to see her. An hour later she arrived in her red V.W. and was taken aback when an official asked to see her credentials.

'Oh dear,' she complained, rummaging in her handbag. 'I've left my press card in my other handbag. You see I changed into a blue dress and that meant changing my bag and shoes — but Mr. Gresham is expecting me. Fraulein Haffner. I'm to interview him.'

Eventually she satisfied the man, and was shown into a room. A few minutes later Nigel arrived. Elisabeth examined him critically and liked what she saw. He was tall and erect, very distinguished, and still handsome. There was a no-nonsense look about him, and along with it a hint of good humour.

'You realise,' Nigel said, sitting down after he had shaken hands with her, 'that there is almost nothing I can tell you that isn't known already? There have been quite a number of these interviews.'

'Yes, but the situation is different now, Mr. Gresham. A letter has been received. We've all been hoping that your son would be released at any moment, and now it seems he is still in danger and is appealing for help.'

'Your English is very good.'

'Not as good as your German, but I thought you might prefer to speak in English. I wanted some personal facts about Mr. Gresham. Mine is, after all, a magazine mainly for women.'

'Quite. What sort of facts?'

'What sort of baby was he?'

'What sort of . . . ?' Nigel stared. 'Small, red-faced, noisy and incredibly ugly. Just like any other.'

'He's an only child?'

'Yes.'

'Was he clever at school?'

'Only at dodging work, so far as I could discover.'

So it went on for a time, as the

curiosity of Elisabeth over Charles's early life was legitimately satisfied.

'I hope you're not going to publish all this rubbish,' Nigel complained, glad to be able to say honestly that he had no photographs of Charles, especially as a baby.

'I'm just trying to get the outline. I shan't publish all of it, but our readers will want to know something about such an interesting personality. Now about romance, Mr. Gresham. When did his passionate love affair with Miss Innescourt begin?'

'His *what*?' Nigel glared.

'I'm sorry, did I say something wrong? He is engaged to Miss Innescourt, isn't he?'

'So I understand.'

'Didn't he tell you?'

'No, it was some sort of secret I gather. I didn't find out till after he'd been kidnapped.'

'You know Miss Innescourt, of course? And her parents?'

'Yes, I've met the family.'

'It's a suitable marriage?'

'I don't know what you mean,' Nigel snapped.

'Well, you're pleased about it?'

'If it's what he wants,' Nigel said, looking anything but pleased. He longed to be able to say that there was no engagement.

'Was he engaged at any time before?'

'Certainly not.'

'Surely he's attractive, isn't he? There must have been other girls.'

'You'll have to ask him about that.'

'So he did not discuss his love life with you?'

'Good God, no!'

Elisabeth hid a smile. This was fun. She asked a few more questions about girls and watched as Nigel grew more and more impatient. Then she changed the subject again.

'What are his plans about business? What will you do when he is released?'

'Go home with him. We have no plans.'

'Is it true that you are opening a

factory here in Carmania?'

'There was talk of it. I haven't had time to think of such things.'

'Of course not, I'm sorry. I was wondering if your son would be returning here on business.'

'He may do.'

'Before he retires?'

Nigel said nothing for a moment, while he studied her. 'Perhaps. As I say, business is taking second place just now.'

'Will you be bringing any more pressure to bear on the Prime Minister to give in to the kidnappers' demands?'

'I've already been in touch with him this morning. There isn't much I can do except to repeat my requests. I believe the Grand Duke is considering the matter.'

'I see. I'm sorry to have had to ask you all these questions at such a difficult time. Unfortunately it's my job.'

'Oh it's all right, I understand.' He sat back and looked at her appraisingly, and liked what he saw. She had a nice face, a face which mirrored a thoroughly nice nature. She was very attractive of course, with a lovely figure and long slim legs. She wore a smart blue dress, very business-like, and he liked her voice. All of which was of particular interest at the moment.

'What's your real name?' he asked casually and it was a split second before her jaw dropped.

★ ★ ★

'My name is Trudi Haffner.'

'I don't think so,' Nigel said easily. 'Oh it's all right, I shan't send for the police — yet. I don't think your name is Haffner and I don't think you're German. Certainly you aren't from Bonn — the accent is all wrong. You see, my dear, from 1945 onwards I've spent more time in Germany than out of it, so I can recognise accents. No, I'd say you were Carmanian and that you and your friends kidnapped my son.

How does that sound?'

'I haven't the faintest idea where your son is.'

He looked into those cornflower blue eyes of hers and smiled.

'I see. I believe you, but unfortunately that doesn't answer my question. I didn't ask where he is. Now look here, I can do one of several things. I can call the police and tell them that you were with my son several days ago, *after* he'd been kidnapped. That should interest them. Or we can discuss it sensibly, because there's something very odd going on and I want to know all about it.'

'How did you know?' she asked after a moment's hesitation.

'You asked about his resignation. Charles has never talked about resigning in his life ... until he was kidnapped. He wrote me a private letter, *which you know about*, telling me not to worry, telling me everything was all right, and saying that when he was free he intended to resign. He asked me to keep the letter secret. Only my wife and I know that he wrote at all, never mind what he wrote. So you must have been there. Who are you?'

Elisabeth sighed and then answered. It took quite a long time for there was a lot to tell. Nigel listened to her in silence until her account had ended.

'It was very enterprising of you to come to see me. Why did you do it?' he demanded.

'I was curious to see what Charles's father was like.'

'Curious about Charles, too, judging by all the questions you asked. Was he an obedient child, indeed! So the silly young fool is keeping up the pretence. It must have been a shock to you.'

'It was.'

'You have no idea at all where he might be?'

'The only place Rudi and I could think of was the cottage, but he wasn't there. Everything was so neat and tidy. However he'd been in the village shop yesterday — it must have been him

— and said he was returning to Germany, which means he's moved somewhere.'

'That's true. I agree it seems as though he's left the cottage, but where the devil could he go. I can't think of anywhere. His acquaintances in Carmania are few, and all business ones. Nobody would help him in a mad scheme like this. You'd better come and meet my wife.'

'You aren't going to send for the police?'

'I'll leave that to Charles, if he feels inclined, which it seems he probably doesn't. No, my dear, no police. However you do interest me. Is there something going on between you and Charles?'

'No,' she said, shaking her head.

'Some sort of romantic something?'

She blushed furiously. 'Of course not. We hardly know one another.'

'Damned if I can see what that's got to do with it. He isn't engaged to that Innescourt girl, you know.'

'I know. He told me she had made it all up.'

'She seems to have found a boy friend to comfort her in her distress. Have you met her?'

'I was going to interview her, just to see what she is like.'

'I do admire your spirit,' he chuckled. 'That should be quite an interview. You must promise to give me a full account of it. Come along and meet Nancy, my wife.'

She followed him into their quarters at the back of the embassy and was introduced to Charles's mother. She sat quietly, not quite knowing where to look, while Nigel explained matters to his wife. Nancy got up and stood beside Elisabeth and patted her shoulder.

'I'm very glad to know Charles is in no danger, and I think you're a very brave girl indeed.'

'Brave?'

'Kidnapping people to stop this stupid arms race. I'm sure I'd never have done it. You must bring your brother to meet us. Nigel, can't we all go out for dinner tonight? I want to meet Elisabeth's brother.'

'Good idea. We'll go to Manfred's. They do the best food in town there. Can you manage that, Elisabeth?'

'Yes, but are you sure?' she asked, confused. 'I mean, well, we caused all the trouble.'

'You aren't causing any trouble now, Charles is. We've never had dinner with kidnappers before. You really started something, and now that Charles has sent this latest note there's an absolute panic.'

'You mean in the Government?' Elisabeth asked.

'Yes. This could lead to a constitutional crisis, because His Royal Highness, the Grand Duke, is openly opposed to the Prime Minister, and the country seems to be pretty evenly divided on the issue. The Secretary General of the United Nations has asked for the defence agreement to be shelved for the moment, at least until there can be a referendum on it. Jung is sitting tight, of course. I don't blame him for that. He's a professional politician and they use fences for chairs even in their homes. Do you know, Jung may have to follow the Secretary General's advice after all? We'll see how things develop in the next twenty-four hours. That will give us a clue. Meantime we can all stop worrying — at least you and your brother and my wife and I. Wherever Charles is, he's safe.'

'You're very kind to me,' Elisabeth said falteringly.

'What nonsense my dear,' Nancy Gresham disclaimed. 'We'll make the arrangements for dinner and you and your brother will be our guests tonight. We want to know all about you both.'

When Elisabeth had departed, not quite sure if she was dreaming, Nigel turned to his wife.

'Well, she's a big improvement on Janice Innescourt. I don't think I mind her much as a daughter-in-law, do you?'

'You think there is something between them?'

'I don't pretend to know how the girl feels, but I know how Charles does. Good heavens, Nancy, you can work it out for yourself. Charles has always been very intolerant about having his plans messed about, yet here he is apparently happy as a sandboy at being kidnapped. He's even kept the plot simmering after those young idiots called it off. Why should he be so keen to make Elisabeth's plan work? Charles never took any interest in politics in his life. I shouldn't think he'd care if the Americans built missile bases all over Europe — or didn't build them.

'Then there's this business of retiring. That's the real clincher. He's always been wrapped up in his work, too much so in fact, but that's my fault. Within hours of meeting this girl he wants to retire and change his entire way of life. You're not going to tell me it was because of meeting her brother. It's the girl all right. No, I don't know how she feels, but I'm certain he's fallen for her.'

'I believe you're right. She feels the same way about him, that's clear.'

'Then everything's all right,' Nigel said simply. 'Nice girl.'

'I'm not so sure,' Nancy mused. 'There's something sad about her. I wonder if Charles has told her he loves her. Probably not. You men are so stupid.'

'I told you, didn't I?' her husband protested.

'Only after I'd brought the fact to your notice in a roundabout way,' Nancy said equably. 'If I'd left things to you we'd never have married.'

'Oh,' Nigel answered blankly.

10

Charles sat reading in the sun, wearing nothing but his slacks. His underwear, socks and shirts all hung on the line drying. It was a warm morning, and he was trying to read a book from Elisabeth's collection. His attention kept wandering, this morning, and at last he let the book drop to his lap.

He was not dissatisfied with life. Tension was building up again in the capital, and nobody knew where he was. He had foreseen the possibility of a police visit, and each morning he had tidied up the cottage. He had washed up immediately after every meal and put the dishes away. He buried refuse in a pit he had dug behind the shed which did duty as a garage. Above all he kept a good look out.

He was tolerably pleased with his ability to deceive. When the police had come finally, he had been out in the woods, and had returned to discover their car parked before the cottage, so he'd stayed hidden till they'd gone; then he'd gone into the village and hired the taxi and told a story about going home to Germany. In Borgrad he had hired a self-drive car and bought a transistor radio. It was only when he got back to the cottage that he realised that once again he had forgotten about clothes, so today he was reduced to doing his laundry. It was safe enough. The police wouldn't come back.

He had also watched Elisabeth and Rudi's visit to the cottage, which he had been anticipating for days. He still didn't know why it had taken them so long to come back, but it was no accident that he was out. He rose early and kept away from the cottage as much as possible during daylight. He had a little glade, not far off, where he liked to lie and read. Things were definitely satisfactory. Nobody knew where he was.

He glanced at his watch, got up and stretched, and went inside for the radio. He brought it out to the patch of garden and turned it on. After a few minutes the news started and he noted that he was back in the number one position. Indeed it seemed that he had rarely been anywhere lower than top of the bill since the whole business had started.

Dr. Jung had announced that discussions were taking place with the American Ambassador, the Grand Duke and a representative of the Secretary General of the United Nations, who had arrived in Borgrad that morning in response to the latest development. The talks were secret.

Students and others had staged the biggest demonstration in the country's history, and letters and telephone calls were pouring into the capital from all over the country. Someone had chalked rude signs all over the walls of the American Embassy — a characteristic touch, Charles thought. In most other countries they'd have broken all the windows and probably torn down the railings while they were at it. Carmanian demonstrations were very restrained.

So it went on. A statement from the Prime Minister's office was expected 'hourly'; prayers were being said in all churches for the safety of the missing man; the police and the army once again felt certain that at any moment arrests would be made. They'd been certain of that from the outset — Charles found it an interesting glimpse into the meaning behind official police statements.

It was all according to his plan. The only thing which spoiled what was basically an extremely pleasant arrangement was that Elisabeth had gone. It had been stupid of him, of course, to imagine that she could be interested in him. He was ten years her senior, no handsome film star and he had devoted his adult life to business so that really he knew nothing except how to make money. This was probably the most stupid pursuit of all, for the more you made the more a Government — for which possibly you hadn't voted — took away from you. Elisabeth was young, vivacious, intelligent, full of enthusiasm and burning with a faith of her own — witness the fact that she had literally masterminded the plan to kidnap an Ambassador as a protest against an arms deal. What would a person like that want with a dry stick like himself?

He sighed. He was engaged to a girl he didn't want to marry, and the one girl who had really made him sit up and take notice had gone off and left him, making it pretty clear that she didn't encourage his tentative advances. Which was a tragedy. He'd like to repeat that kiss. He'd like to repeat it many times.

He sighed again and picked up his book. Then he heard the sound of an engine. Quickly and silently he got to his feet and whipped all his washing off the line, pocketing the clothes pegs. He picked up his book and raced indoors.

He gathered up his shoes and was looking round for a hiding place when he heard the car stop. He ran silently into the bedroom, squashed himself into the clothes cupboard and pulled the door shut after him.

It was uncomfortable, crouched in the cupboard with an armful of clothes and shoes, the pegs in his pocket digging into his groin, one hand holding the door closed by the piece of string which was for hanging ties. Who was the caller, he wondered? He could hear footsteps but when he let the door open just a fraction he could see nothing through the crack. After a time the footsteps faded and a little later he heard the car engine again. He gave it a few minutes before coming out. The coast was clear. Police, he thought — or a policeman, anyway. Who else could it be? Maybe it was some soldier or policeman who didn't know that the cottage had been searched already.

Charles hung out the washing again and stood outside debating whether or not to make some coffee. He heard and saw nothing until it was too late. Then a voice behind him said, 'So, you are here after all. I suspected it.'

He whirled, open mouthed, and saw a man, a little younger than himself, with very fair hair. He wore a neat dark business suit which was oddly out of place in these sylvan surroundings.

'What do you want?' Charles asked sharply.

'You, you imposter. You are Charles Gresham, aren't you, and you are here, where I guessed you were.'

'All right. Who are you?' Charles demanded coolly.

'My name is Kurt Schwarz. Does it mean anything to you?'

'No, should it?'

'Miss Renner did not mention me?'

'Not so far as I recall. You must be one of the gang, the Neutrality Committee or whatever it is called.

'Correct. And you have been making love to Elisabeth Renner.'

Charles wondered if his ears had let

him down. 'I've been doing *what?*' he asked.

'Making love to Elisabeth. Oh don't deny it. I know everything. How do you think I knew you were here?'

'I've no idea. How did you know?'

'Because when Elisabeth refused to marry me I knew there must be another man. Then, when she said she didn't know where you were, that you were still a prisoner, I wondered. That didn't sound true and suddenly I guessed the truth. She did know where you were, and there was another man — you, Mr. Gresham! Well, you shan't have her.'

'Oh, shan't I?' Charles replied, stung by this remark.

'No, because I forbid it. How would you like me to go to the police, Mr. Gresham, and tell them that you and Elisabeth have been hoaxing them?'

'Don't be stupid,' Charles snapped.

'Who is being stupid? I am a school teacher. I am not stupid. You will do as I say, or else . . .'

'For goodness sake, grow up. You're talking like an idiot.'

'Do you dare to call me an idiot, you stupid Englishman? Me, Kurt Schwarz! I tell you I shall be the youngest headmaster in all Carmania soon.'

'What a ghastly thought. You're talking absolute rubbish. Elisabeth has no idea where I am.'

'Ho ho,' Schwarz laughed bitterly. 'She has no idea, and yet I can lay hands on you when I want. What a lie. You're having an affair with my girl.'

'Suppose I am?' Charles demanded, his temper rising.

'You admit it then?'

'I'm admitting nothing ... I'm simply saying that it's none of your damned business.'

'It is my business. I chose Elisabeth as my wife a very long time ago, and I shall not permit her to waste herself on a philanderer.'

'Steady on,' Charles said, relenting. He felt rather sorry for the ridiculous school teacher. 'Elisabeth will do her own choosing, and I'm not a philanderer. Now, if you've got anything to say, why don't you go and see Elisabeth?'

'I shall, don't you worry, but first I shall thrash you to teach you a lesson.'

'Good lord, don't be silly.'

'Then promise that you will never see Elisabeth again.'

'I shall promise no such thing.'

'I demand that you leave the country immediately, without seeing Elisabeth, do you hear?'

'Now look here, whatever your name is, I'm trying to help Elisabeth and her friends, of whom I presume you are one. So just go away and leave me alone. If you want the plan to stop the arms deal to succeed, say nothing to anyone for a few days.'

'Do you expect me to help you?' Kurt asked bitterly. 'You are trying to steal my girl. Very well then, I shall report you to the police. I shall tell them where you are, then you will be forced to leave the country. I'll phone from Rindt and I'll get help there also. You'll be cornered here, alone. I'll tell them that you're a practical joker. They'll fine you and deport you. Do you hear?'

'You must be out of your mind.' Charles stared at the furious teacher in disbelief. 'If the police find me here at Elisabeth's cottage, she'll be implicated and so will Rudi.'

'We'll say you broke in. If you try to involve Elisabeth and her brother, the rest of us will give them an alibi.'

'What sort of rubbish have you been reading? The police would never believe a tale like that.'

'Then go away.'

'No I won't. You go away. Go back to school and play with the other children, and keep your big mouth shut.'

That did it. Kurt flung himself on Charles and knocked him over. As Charles staggered to his feet the maddened Kurt rained a hail of blows on him.

'Oh damn,' Charles said and stepped

to one side and unleashed a right hook.

A glazed expression came over Kurt's eyes, and his knees began to sag. Charles hit him once more, and he went out like a light.

Then, as he stood over the inert figure on the grass, he remembered what Kurt Schwarz had said. Elisabeth had refused to marry him. That was very interesting. Charles was glad about that.

★ ★ ★

The news bulletins were of a depressing sameness, yet tension was still mounting. Meetings were in progress, a statement was expected 'at any moment now', the public were informed of the comings and goings at the American Embassy, the Prime Minister's office, the Prime Minister's home and even at the royal palace. It was obvious to everyone that it was going to be a close thing, whatever was decided.

Rudi and Elisabeth were at home this

evening, and Elisabeth was making veal stuffed with pâté for their evening meal. It was somewhat less luxurious than the magnificent spread they had had with Nigel and Nancy Gresham the previous evening, but when it had been garnished with chopped parsley and wedges of lemon, and was served up with peas and green salad, it looked good enough to Rudi.

'You'll make some man a fine wife,' he remarked. 'If I'd met even one girl who could cook like you, I'd have married years ago.'

'You never give your girl friends a chance to cook,' Elisabeth retorted. 'That's your trouble.'

'The fact is that I'm spoiled at home. I'm going to miss you.'

'I'm not going anywhere.'

'No? Aren't you? I wonder.'

'Now what does that mean?' Elisabeth asked, staring.

'Well you were pretty friendly with Charles's parents last night.'

'They were very kind to us.'

'Agreed, but especially to you. It would be nice to visit you in England. I expect you'll stay in England.'

'Rudi!'

'I'm sorry,' he apologised unconvincingly, 'but you are in love with Charles Gresham and I'm not so sure he's going to get away from you.'

'He'll have forgotten all about me by now.'

'I wonder, Liz. I wonder. Tell me about that girl who said she was engaged to him. You didn't tell me much yesterday.'

Elisabeth thought back to the previous afternoon and smiled. It had been an amusing 'interview'. Janice had no objection to being interviewed by a supposed journalist from a German women's mazagine, but she had been a little embarrassed by the presence of Count Johannes von Galland and had explained at least four times that he was simply a friend she had met here in the hotel who was standing by her through her ordeal. Elisabeth's first feeling had been of dismay, for the regally beautiful and elegantly dressed Janice was like something from the pages of a high class fashion magazine or society journal. How on earth could Charles, or any man, be indifferent to such a woman?

After a few moments however, the first impression began to fade a little. Janice was incapable of not being condescending. Soon Elisabeth became amused. She decided that Charles had been very long suffering.

As she recalled the occasion for Rudi they began to chuckle and then to laugh. It had its amusing aspects which appealed to them both.

'It doesn't sound to me,' Rudi said, pushing back his plate and wiping his mouth with his napkin, 'as though she's pining much for Charles. Who is this Count von Galland?'

'I've never heard of him, but he was looking at her with great calf's eyes. I think he may be a few years younger than she is, and his English isn't terribly good, so probably he doesn't realise how snobbish she is — or else he's the same. He was very well dressed. Perhaps he's rich.'

'He's got a title, even if only a Baratavian one,' Rudi said dryly. 'Perhaps she likes that. Charles would be amused if he knew that you had gone to see Miss Innescourt.'

'Charles will probably never find out. I don't suppose he'll come to visit us.'

'I can't help feeling you do him an injustice. I wish I knew where he was.'

'So do I,' Elisabeth exclaimed and her brother gave her a sympathetic smile.

He sat reading after dinner but an idea kept nagging away at the back of his mind and at last he put his book down.

'I think I'll go out.'

'So late?'

'It's only a quarter to ten. I feel like a drive. Don't wait up for me. I'm restless this evening.'

'All right then. I'm going to bed

early. I woke very early this morning.'

'Then I'll see you tomorrow. It was a lovely supper, Liz — as always.'

He kissed her cheek and went outside, started his car and drove through the city. The streets were quiet in the darkness and he headed southeast on the main autobahn. At Baltz he began the winding ascent of the mountain road. He parked the car in among some bushes and completed the last hundred yards of his journey on foot. As he drew near the cottage he smiled. There were lights. His guess hadn't been so far out after all.

Charles heard nothing until the door was pushed open. He jumped to his feet alarmed, and then relaxed a little when he recognised Rudi.

'So you've caught me. Come in. I can offer you coffee, chocolate or cocoa.'

'Nothing thanks. We were here before, looking for you.'

'I know. I saw you. The police have been here too.'

'I didn't see where else you could be.

When I thought more about it, it had to be here. You might stay away during daylight, but I was pretty sure you would sleep here.'

'Quite right. I wasn't as clever as I thought. I've had another caller, name of Kurt Schwarz. A friend of yours.'

'He came here? Why?'

'Looking for me. It's quite a story. It seems Elisabeth told him that you didn't know where I was now, and that I was acting on my own. This struck him as odd, and then when she refused to marry him he jumped to the conclusion that it was all a blind, and that I was having an affair with her. So he came straight up here to see what he could find out, and caught me red handed. I had to knock him out and tie him up.'

'Kurt? What on earth for?'

'Well may you ask. He lost his head completely. First he demanded that I leave the country at once, and I refused because it seems to me that we're on the point of winning this particular war we're fighting. This is no time for me to turn up in Borgrad. Then he said he would go to the police and have me arrested, and that they'd find me here alone and treat it as a hoax, and gaol me or deport me or something. Of course the first thing they'd do is find out whose cottage this is, but the silly fool wouldn't listen to reason, and in the end he went for me — so I bopped him and tied him up. He's in the other bedroom, tied to the bed. I've fed him. As a matter of fact I've been wondering what the blazes to do with him.'

Rudi burst out laughing and it was some time before he calmed down.

'It's so funny,' he exlained. 'Poor Kurt, I'm afraid he took it for granted that Liz would marry him. I can just picture him giving you an ultimatum, and then trying to fight you. He's no warrior.'

'I could see that. Neither am I. What am I to do with him, Rudi?'

'Perhaps I'd better have some coffee. Let's go into the kitchen.'

They sat at the kitchen table while the coffee percolated, and discussed plans. In the end they agreed that it would be better to keep Kurt where he was, but Rudi would have a talk with him before he left.

'How are things in Borgrad?' Charles asked. 'Any more demonstrations?'

'No, not today, but everyone seems to think that the defence agreement will be called off.'

'I have a plan,' Charles said slowly. 'Now that you've caught up with me, we might be able to help things along. Listen and I'll tell you.'

It was 4 a.m. before Rudi left. They had found a great deal to discuss.

11

'Who?' Jason McCudden asked.

'A Rudolf Renner, sir. He says it is most important and confidential. He seems decent enough, but he flatly refused to give details. He said to say *Busol*.'

'*Busol*? How did he know that name? I wouldn't have thought anyone in Carmania would know it. It's only recently off the secret list.'

Busol was the name of the latest atomic missile, which would be sited in Carmania. Details had most definitely not been announced. Charles's inspired guess about it had been right. 'Very well, let him in.'

Rudi, a little red-eyed but otherwise smart and brisk, entered and sat down.

'What's this about *Busol*? Where did you hear of it?'

'It isn't a secret is it?' Rudi asked,

raising his eyebrows. 'It's your new missile.'

Jason looked at him suspiciously. He still didn't understand where some non-official Carmanian had picked up the name. 'What do you want?'

'It's about Charles Gresham. I wanted to talk about that. He feels you should build your missile sites in some other country.'

'*He* feels? Have you see him?'

'Yes, but don't press any buttons. You see Gresham was never kidnapped at all.'

'Are you drunk?'

'No, Mr. Ambassador. Gresham staged his own kidnapping. He hired some youngsters to put on a show outside your embassy, and he went into hiding. He's been camping in the mountains where the police won't find him, and he's got some young boy whose name I don't know and which Gresham won't reveal, who gets him food and delivers messages. Gresham is fairly wealthy, you realise.'

'Yes, of course. I don't believe you, friend. Not one word. You'd better talk fast before I get the police round here.'

'It won't do any good,' Rudi warned. 'I shan't talk. Besides, I'm just a messenger. Gresham has got this thing about the atomic build-up. Personally I think he's a little crazy — on this subject anyway. The point is that he's written a letter and he's arranged with someone — and don't ask me who — that in the event of his death copies will be delivered to various people . . . for publication.'

'Why should he die?'

'He's going to commit suicide tomorrow morning, right in the middle of the city, as a protest against your defence agreement. He means it. I told you, he staged this whole kidnapping himself. Imagine it, an important man like Mr. Gresham.'

'I met him. He looked sane enough to me.'

'I expect he is on other subjects,' Rudi agreed. 'I only spent an hour or two with him. I don't even know where he's hiding. He came out just to see me. So please don't try pushing me about, Mr. McCudden. I'm doing my best to help.'

'Who are you anyway?' Jason McCudden began to cross-examine Rudi and the answers were all straightforward and satisfactory.

'You think he'll commit suicide?' Jason demanded.

'I know it. He says he has a gun. In the middle of the city, when it's busy, who can stop him? A man steps out of a doorway into the street, pulls a trigger, and bang — you've got a dead body and letters of protest against the U.S.A.'

'Why do they always pick on America?' Jason grumbled. 'Dr. Jung was just wild to get the atomic bases in Carmania. We've got good relations here.'

'I know,' Rudi sympathised, straight-faced. 'Some people are never satisfied. There you are. I've done what I promised and now it's up to you.'

'Hey wait, don't go.'

They sat and talked for another twenty minutes, but in truth there was really nothing to say. At last Rudi went. The first thing Jason did was to check that there was a Rudi Renner, an electronics engineer, who lived at the address Rudi had given. While the details were being confirmed, the Ambassador thought grimly. The talks were on the verge of a breakdown anyway. He himself now held the power to make the final decision. There had been some quick work, and alternative sites had been found in another country, just in case.

Jason McCudden weighed up all the pressures, and all the arguments pro and con. He was due at the Prime Minister's office at noon for a last talk, to settle the matter one way or the other. During the past thirty-six hours he had been more and more inclined towards calling off the whole thing. It wasn't worth all the fuss, and the American image was taking its customary beating in certain quarters. Jason had long realised that there is no justice in these matters, but he saw no point in providing ammunition for America's detractors.

'We'll pull out,' he muttered angrily. 'To hell with them all. Just let the war start up again and see who they holler for!' He scowled ferociously at his blotting pad and waited. The news, when it came, was that Rudi Renner was a genuine person unconnected with any political or other groups. He had a girl friend, a sister, liked classical music, and that was about all one could say about Rudi Renner.

Jason made up his mind. There would be no messy suicide, leaving notes saying, 'Uncle Sam drove me to it'.

He began to draft a long memo to the Secretary of State, which would be the basis of his definitive report on the entire affair. It helped to pass the time.

Another less important crisis was taking place in the grounds of a hotel not very far from the embassy. Janice

Innescourt and Count Johannes faced one another and their destiny. Janice sat on a rustic bench, hands neatly folded in her lap, and looked soulfully at the intense young nobleman who had just offered her his hand, his heart, the ancestral vineyards and the title of countess. There was nothing Janice would like more than to be a countess to her mother's mere 'Lady'. Being rich would have been satisfactory, but to have money *and* a superior title — that was simply divine.

'Dear Johannes,' she murmured, patting his hand absent-mindedly, 'I shall have to break the news to Charles Gresham of course. Poor Charles, to have endured so much and then at the end of it all to lose the woman in his life. It's so tragic.'

'You agree then?' Johannes asked eagerly. He thought of last year's balance sheet. Unfortunately Baratavia was not a wine producing country, any more than England was, and although the von Gallands had been wine producers for a century, it was not good wine. In recent years the demand had dropped alarmingly. With the wealth of an English milord, he thought, the family fortunes could be restored. Wait till his aged father discovered how clever he had been.

'Dear Johannes,' Janice repeated. 'How can I resist you?'

She permitted him to kiss her hand, and then her cheek, before disengaging herself.

'We must say nothing yet,' she warned. 'The world sees me as the fiancée of Charles Gresham, waiting for him to be released by those wretched kidnappers. It wouldn't look good if they discovered that I had got myself engaged to someone else while waiting.'

'No, no,' Johannes agreed, 'but our arrangement is definite.'

'Indeed it is. I expect they're going to give in over those wretched missiles at any time now, and when I see Charles I shall break our news to him. Then I think we had better fly to England and announce the engagement there. You'll come to England with me?'

'I should love to come to England with you, to meet your parents, to see your ancestral home.'

'How charming. You say the right thing always. I like emeralds.'

'Pardon?' he asked, puzzled.

'Emeralds. An engagement ring of one large emerald set in lots of diamonds.'

'But of course.'

'And perhaps an emerald and dia- mond necklace to match? For evening wear? I do like sets of things, don't you?'

Johannes swallowed, and then forced a smile. After all, one had to lay out a little money on occasion. It would be an expense well worth it. 'For you, only the best,' he murmured, squeezing her hand.

'Countess Janice von Galland. It sounds nice, don't you think?'

'Like music,' he assured her happily. 'Like divinely inspired music. How happy I am, Janice my love.'

Janice thought fleetingly of Charles and then dismissed him finally from her mind. He had always been a little imperious and abrupt, and far too wrapped up in business and other non-essential matters which she believed could safely be left to lesser beings.

Johannes showed an admirable tendency to hang on her every word, and to anticipate her every wish, that had been distressingly lacking in other men, including Charles Gresham. Charles had his factories, he'd be all right.

At the same time, in the British Embassy, Nigel Gresham was studying some mail which had arrived from England. One of the difficulties of having created a small industrial empire was that, like other sorts of rulers of whatever importance, he had very little privacy. Life was one series of unwelcome intrusions. This time, however, the word unwelcome did not apply. He found Nancy in their bedroom. 'What would you say if I gave up business?' he demanded.

'Go and see a doctor?' she suggested.

'No, I'm serious my dear. Could you stand having me about the place?'

'I've no idea, Nigel. It's so long since it last happened. What is all this about?'

'Well, you know Charles wants to pull out.'

'Very sensible of him, I thought. If he marries that lovely girl, Elisabeth, and settles down at home, he will be very happy.'

'By a strange coincidence an American group, with whom I've done a lot of business, are making a take-over bid. I've known about the possibility for some time, and I was going to resist on principle. Now I'm not so sure. It's a good offer. I'm inclined not to fight it.'

'Let me understand, my dear,' his wife said patiently. 'If you don't fight it, whatever that means, some Americans will take away your companies?'

'They'll pay. I'll get cash and shares.'

'I see. Will that make you rich?'

'It will, rather,' he smiled. 'They'll offer me a job of some sort, following

251

the take-over, but I don't want one. The same would happen to Charles. They'd offer to keep him on, but I imagine he'll refuse that. What will happen is that Charles and I will have a great deal of money in cash and shares, and a disgustingly large income, and no jobs. No houses either, except the flat in London which presumably we'd sell. Oh, and no cars. We'll have to buy a house and a car and settle down somewhere.'

'Near Wells?' Nancy asked, thinking at once of her birthplace. 'I've always wanted to go back there. It's so peaceful.'

'Anywhere you like. I'd have no office, no business trips, darling. I'd be under your feet.'

'Not for long, my dear. I expect you'd buy the cathedral or something.'

'Turn it into a profitable concern, you mean? It's an idea but I doubt if they'd sell. No, I'd quit. I'll take up fishing or something. How does it sound to you?'

'I'll risk it,' his wife smiled. 'Think how nice it would be if we found out we liked one another after forty years of marriage.'

'Is it really forty?' he asked.

'Next year in May. Yes, all right Nigel, I'd be rather relieved if you sold out. You're getting too old to chase around the world all the time, and we have far too much money anyway. Perhaps we could both take up fishing.'

He kissed her and patted her shoulder.

'You've been a patient woman. I'll drop them a line in Chicago and tell them how matters stand and then I'll let my own board know. It will be quite a surprise for Charles when he comes home.'

'I wonder when that will be,' Nancy sighed.

'Not long now, I shouldn't think.'

*   *   *

The announcement was made in a special broadcast at three o'clock. As

Charles had cleverly foreseen, neither Jason McCudden nor Dr. Bruno Jung, who had been admitted to the secret, had any intention of letting anyone know that they had been hoaxed by an eccentric, possibly mad, Englishman. The farce of the kidnapping would be played out to the bitter end.

The Carmanian National Anthem was played, and then there was an official announcement to the effect that the defence agreement with the United States had been mutually terminated in view of the obvious feeling in Carmania against it, combined with the kidnapping of the unfortunate Englishman. The missile bases would be sited elsewhere and the U.S. Government had already made the appropriate arrangements. Then Bruno Jung was introduced.

He was quite a performer in public, was Dr. Jung. He spoke movingly about his distress over Charles Gresham, and no one listening could have guessed that Dr. Jung bitterly regretted that circumstances prevented him from burning this pestiferous Englishman at the stake, or boiling him in oil. He couldn't quite make up his mind which he would prefer. One would have thought that Dr. Jung's own son was in jeopardy.

He and his advisers, and His Royal Highness the Grand Duke, had deliberated for a long time and had had full and frank discussions with the American Ambassador. He was glad to say that thanks to American co-operation it had been possible to cancel the previous arrangement without any great inconvenience or any loss of friendship between the two countries. In short all was well that ended well. Dr. Jung closed on a highly emotional note. He beseeched the kidnappers to release Charles Gresham at once, and promised them amnesty. He regarded this last bit as politically cunning. It would strike a responsive chord in the breasts of the Carmanian people, none of whom would ever know that there were no kidnappers anyway. It was that most prized of all political manoeuvres — a gesture which literally cost nothing.

It was only a short time before Dr. Jung realised the full extent of the flood he had released. Telephone calls began at once, to be followed by letters and finally by demonstrations of triumph in various towns and villages. It seemed that almost everyone now felt that Carmania had done the right thing. Meantime people waited for the kidnappers to complete the joy of the occasion by delivering up their victim, hopefully unharmed.

Elisabeth, who had been listening to the radio while doing some ironing, could hardly believe her ears. Rudi arrived in his car shortly after the broadcast, having managed to get the rest of the afternoon off. They hugged one another wildly.

'It worked,' she said gaily. 'It really worked. Oh Rudi, I'd never have guessed it would. Charles did it all.'

'Not a bit of it,' her brother

contradicted. 'You started it all. Without you, none of this would have happened, none of it.'

'I wonder if the police will ever find out what really did happen,' she said, for she knew nothing yet of her brother's visit to Charles at the cottage, and his subsequent visit to Jason McCudden.

'Never,' Rudi said confidently. 'Anyway, we've got an amnesty, so we're safe.'

'I know, isn't it wonderful? Who'd have guessed it?'

Rudi hid a smile. 'Who indeed?'

'Oh if only Charles would come to see us. I'd like to hear the rest of the story. Do you think we dare go to see him, Rudi?'

'I don't know,' he answered, looking convincingly worried. 'He's a pretty important person and when he returns to the city he'll be very busy. I expect the Grand Duke will want to see him, and there are his parents and that Innescourt girl. Probably there's business too. He came here to build a factory. He'll have

257

many things to attend to. What does it matter?'

Elisabeth's face clouded over. 'You're right,' she agreed a little dejectedly. 'Why should he have time for us now? He's done what he intended to do — won our point for us. I'm very grateful to him.'

'So you should be,' Rudi assured her. 'So you should be. It's a real happy ending.'

'Yes,' Elisabeth said, but she was thinking of Charles Gresham. If only she could see him once more. After all, she was a friend of his mother and father now. As she thought of that her heart beat faster. They'd invite her round to meet Charles, of course. That was it. They'd be bound to do that.

'The others will all be proud of you — Kurt, Hans, Willi, all of them.'

'I don't want the credit. I was willing to give up after three days.'

Rudi hugged her. 'I know you can't claim any credit in public, that you'll never get the recognition you deserve because it's all a secret — and neither will Charles, come to that — but to those of us who know, you're a real heroine. Think of the risks you took.'

She laughed suddenly. 'We'd all have been in prison a long time ago if Charles hadn't been the sort of person he is,' she replied. 'I think we had better just forget the whole thing now.'

Rudi went out to buy a bottle of champagne because it was, after all, a very special occasion. He drank comparatively little and Elisabeth did not drink at all, but tonight they would toast one another and their victory. When he had gone she turned back to finish her little bit of ironing and she paused with the iron in her hand.

It was going to be difficult, she realised, to adjust to the humdrum life again. It had been an intensely exciting period during which many things had happened. Even if she hadn't fallen in love with Charles Gresham, it would still have been stimulating. Now a curious flatness of spirit fell on her.

She'd always been happy and content in the past, but as she viewed the prospect of cooking, washing, ironing, working, waiting for the annual holiday or a week-end picnic, or the weekly music night, she felt depressed. It no longer satisfied her.

She was almost feeling sorry for herself when Rudi returned with the champagne. Indeed it was such an anticlimax that she had to go to her bedroom for a little time while she shed a few tears.

12

Kurt Schwarz was no longer tied. He stood uncertainly facing Charles, remembering the hot, scathing words of Rudi Renner, uttered late last night. Rudi had not been polite to him. Now they had listened to the Prime Minister's broadcast and Charles had untied his hands and the hobble on his feet.

'You can go now, Kurt,' Charles said mildly. 'I'm sorry I had to tie you up but I couldn't risk your going to the police and spoiling everything.'

'I suppose you think I'm a fool,' Kurt blurted out.

'No.' Charles shook his head. 'I don't think so. When a man's disappointed in love, he doesn't stop to think. But that doesn't make him a fool.'

Kurt rubbed his wrists and then turned away. At the corner of the cottage he turned back.

'I suppose you think you're some sort of hero?' he demanded.

Charles shook his head again. 'No, I just helped a little with your plans.'

Indeed, he ruminated as Kurt disappeared from sight, he was no hero. In fact he was heartily glad, now, that the whole affair was over. He had business to attend to, really important business, nothing to do with mere atomic missiles and the possibility of nuclear war.

He tidied up in the cottage for the last time, buried the last of the refuse, and then left, closing the door behind him. He locked it and put the key under the stone where it was usually kept. He got out the car, and drove into Borgrad. He wore his dark glasses and his shapeless tweed hat. The first thing he did was to return the car to the hire firm and get back the balance of his deposit, then he set off on foot for the British Embassy. He walked inside and went to the receptionist.

'I'd like to see Mr. and Mrs. Gresham. I believe they're staying with the Ambassador.'

'Whom shall I say, sir?'

'Charles Gresham.'

The girl almost jumped clean out of her seat. She did things with keys and spoke into an intercom.

'Yes that's right, Charles Gresham. He's here.'

An agitated Ambassador and an even more agitated First Secretary arrived on the scene.

'Look here, I'm all right. I just want to see my parents.'

'Of course, of course,' Hugh Maddox agreed. 'So you shall. Now, are you sure you don't need a doctor?'

'Quite certain. I haven't been ill-treated.'

'Then I'll take you to your parents, but you realise we must inform the Prime Minister, and of course the Chief of Police, and there will be reporters too.'

'Yes, yes,' Charles nodded. 'I under-stand.'

He was taken to the residential part

of the building, to the suite occupied by his parents. Nancy let out a cry of joy and hugged him, and when he got the chance Nigel shook his hand warmly. They talked non-stop for half an hour while they drank tea. After that Charles was summoned to meet Police Chief Braun.

Hugh Maddox, who was completely in the dark like everyone else, and who remained so, never knew why Braun was so off-hand. Braun had been briefed by the Prime Minister, of course, after being sworn to complete silence. Only three men would ever know the whole truth — McCudden, Jung and Braun. The search was to be called off. No enquiries were to be made into the kidnapping. There had been *no* kidnapping. It was a hoax. Go through the motions, and that was literally all.

Braun tried not to glare at Charles.

'You are well, Mr. Gresham?'

'Oh absolutely,' Charles beamed. He guessed that Braun must know the whole truth.

'Now, about your kidnappers . . . '

'Ah yes. When they drove me away from the embassy that day they switched cars in a part of the city I don't know. A new lot took over, all wearing masks and drove me out of town in a big American car. I was blindfolded.'

'American car?'

'Yes, a Cadillac.'

'No Carmanians own Cadillacs and none has been stolen. Only the Americans here have Cadillacs, Mr. Gresham.' Braun could not help himself. If Charles was going to tell lies, as undoubtedly he was, let them be reasonable ones.

'Yes, but were they Carmanians? I'm not sure. I never heard any names and they wore masks every time I saw them, but their accents weren't Carmanian.'

'Were they young or old?'

'I don't really know.'

So it went on, the story of how he had been driven, blindfolded, to some place of concealment, kept prisoner in a comfortable room, well fed and well looked after, until today when he was blindfolded again and dropped near the ornamental fountain in the centre of the city. He had come straight to the British Embassy because he knew his parents were there. He had heard all the news broadcasts while in captivity.

What it all boiled down to was the fact that he did not know who had kidnapped him, did not know where he had been, and could not help the police. The entire interview lasted perhaps twenty minutes while Braun asked a few questions which it was absolutely necessary to ask. Then Braun left, privately cursing at having had to waste time going through this charade when there had been an outbreak of house breaking which demanded all his attention.

The whole story, unsatisfactory as it was, had to be repeated for the benefit of the journalists. Its very unsatisfactoriness created an atmosphere of mystery which went down well with the report-ers. Only Hugh Maddox considered that the police had shown too little interest and noticed a few apparent discrepan-cies in Charles's story. That was the business of the police, however, not his. He had no doubt that Charles had been kidnapped and held hostage, and assumed merely that he knew a little more than he wanted to reveal — perhaps because he had been threatened. Maddox was glad to have the affair over and done with. It was always a nuisance when foreigners interfered with British sub-jects, and he had been badgered for days by the Foreign Secretary.

As soon as the brief news of Charles's release was announced pub-licly, Janice Innescourt arrived at the embassy. Normally Janice would have waited for Charles to rush to her side, but circumstances were not normal. In the first place Charles knew very well that they had never been engaged and might be a little huffy over the way she had taken the initiative; and secondly and more importantly, it was essential to wriggle out of the engagement she herself had created so that she could clinch matters with Johannes before he had a chance to change his mind. As soon as she heard the news she booked two flights to London for the next day and took a taxi to the embassy. Charles saw her in a private room.

'Oh darling,' she exclaimed, kissing him on the lips lightly. 'How glad I am to see you safe. Are you all right, Charles dear?'

'Never better.' Charles was wondering just how to handle her. She would be furious to learn that they were not engaged and not going to become so in future.

'I was so worried about you. I rushed to this dreadful country and I've been waiting here day after day.'

'I know, I had a radio. I heard all the broadcasts.'

She gave him a nervous smile. 'You're not angry with me, are you Charles dear?'

'No, not angry.'

'You see, the reporters got the wrong idea. They seemed to think we were engaged and before I knew what was happening it was too late to contradict them. I mean, it would have looked pretty odd if I'd started to issue denials when you were in danger of your life, wouldn't it?'

'Uh, yes.' Charles's ears pricked up. Was it possible that Janice was actually trying to wriggle off her own hook? If so, why?

'So I didn't contradict them. I knew you'd understand.'

'I do,' Charles agreed, watching her like a hawk for some tell tale sign.

'I was so worried about you. You've no idea.'

'I was all right. They treated me very well.'

'The fiends. They should be punished,' she exclaimed indignantly. 'Charles . . . '

'Yes?' he encouraged as she hesitated.

'About the engagement.'

'Yes?' Damned if he'd help her, he thought.

'It wasn't true was it?'

'Not exactly. I did wonder, when I heard the news, if I'd ever said anything to make you think we were engaged,' he replied.

'No!' the word came out like a shot from a gun, and he put his hand to his mouth. It was going to be easy after all.

'I'm so glad. I wouldn't like to deceive you.'

'You see, Charles, there's someone — someone you don't know about.'

The devil there is, he thought. Miracles will never cease. She's pulled it off at last. Well, good luck to her. She deserves it.

'I understand. He wants to marry you?'

'That's exactly it.' She was relieved by his calm manner.

'Then he must do so. I'll leave it to you to make the announcement, shall I? You can tell the press that we've talked it over and changed our minds and that you've found someone else.'

'I thought it might be better to go to

England and just quietly announce the other engagement in *The Times*.'

'What a very sensible idea, Janice. Who is this lucky fellow?'

'Count von Galland.'

'A count? Your parents will be delighted I'm sure.'

'They don't know yet. Johannes and I will fly to London tomorrow and then surprise them all at home.'

'A splendid idea. You must let me buy you an engagement present. What's more I insist on an invitation to the wedding.'

'You darling,' she said with real affection and kissed him again. 'I'm so glad it's all right. I was going to break it to you very gently, but when Johannes asked me to marry him . . . '

'Exactly,' Charles sympathised. 'Something had to be done.'

'I wish you could meet Johannes. He's very charming. His family own vineyards in Baratavia. They've been in the family for centuries. His father is a Chamberlain of Honour to Prince

Conrad of Baratavia, you know.'

'How interesting. Port and pantaloons.'

'What?'

'Nothing Janice. Just a passing thought. I do hope you're going to be happy.'

'Oh I shall,' she forecast, accurately as it turned out later.

When she had gone Charles walked slowly back to join his parents. He picked up the telephone and asked for the First Secretary. When that gentleman had been routed out, and confirmed that he was the general dogsbody in the small embassy, Charles put his question about Baratavian wine. The First Secretary, who fancied himself as a *bon viveur*, laughed.

'Baratavian wine? There is such a thing. You can buy it in the supermarkets here. It costs the equivalent of about thirty pence a bottle and is absolutely foul. I wouldn't touch it if I were you, old chap. The ought to put a label on the bottles saying 'Free from Grapes'.'

'Is there much of it?'

'No, luckily. There's one small vineyard — it belongs to some impoverished and decaying aristocratic family I believe. I'm afraid I don't know the name.'

'It doesn't matter. I was just curious. Thank you very much for your advice.'

Charles hung up with a smile.

'What was that about?' Nigel asked.

Obligingly Charles told him.

★　★　★

'What about Elisabeth?' Nancy Gresham asked after dinner. 'I think you're behaving very badly, Charles.'

'Give me a chance. I've only been back a few hours.'

'She's the first person you should have seen.'

'You don't understand, Mama. I don't want to implicate her, amnesty or no amnesty. Bruno Jung is going to be pretty vindictive for some time, and the less he knows the better. At the moment he thinks I wasn't kidnapped at all, and I want to keep it that way.'

He changed the subject abruptly.

'It's really rather pleasant that you were able to meet Elisabeth and Rudi and have dinner with them. After all, they're going to be part of the family from now on,' he said with a twinkle.

'You haven't seen Elisabeth since they left you in that cottage,' his mother insisted. 'I think you ought to go to their house. If you went after dark, how would the Prime Minister ever find out?'

'It isn't worth the risk. I'm seeing her very soon. In fact I have to go away in a few minutes.'

'Go where?'

'To pack a case and drive to the airport.'

They looked mystified so he smiled and explained, and then went off. Half an hour later he left the embassy without explaining to the Ambassador where he was going, and took a taxi to the airport. It had begun to drizzle again, another wet summer's night. Well, the weather certainly didn't matter. He went to the booking office and spoke to the girl.

Yes, two tickets had been purchased and were awaiting collection. They had been paid for. Charles showed his passport and took the tickets, then asked the girl to cancel the provisional bookings for the next two nights which he knew Rudi would have made. He glanced at his watch. Checking in in fifteen minutes. He was early. He knew the flight would not be full — the night flight to Frankfurt never was, not from Borgrad. He walked over to the news stand, bought a couple of magazines, and sat down to wait.

In the meantime Elisabeth was having surprises of her own. She and Rudi had gone out to a little restaurant to eat, and Rudi had insisted on going home almost immediately after dinner. When they were inside the flat he took her hands and squeezed them.

'Now I want you to pack a suitcase.

Quickly. We have to go.'

'What are you talking about, Rudi?' she demanded.

'Never mind, just do what I say. I have to get you out of this house tonight.'

Her first thought was that somehow she was in trouble over the kidnapping, but she could not see just how this was. She started to argue.

'Please,' Rudi interrupted. 'Just trust me, Liz. You know you can. Go and pack a suitcase with your clothes and things, as though you were going away for a holiday. Do it quickly. To please me. It really is urgent and very important.'

Baffled, she packed. No one but Rudi could have persuaded her to do so without giving a better explanation. Something was wrong, obviously, something important, as he kept insisting, but what?

When she had finished her packing he handed her her coat. She put it on and picked up her handbag while he took the case.

'We must go now.'

'Where?' she demanded.

'A surprise. There's nothing to worry about.'

She shrugged and raised her eyes in a gesture. She would have to humour him. He took her down to his car and set off through the city. It was some time before she realised that they were on the airport road.

'Are you going to the airport?' she demanded suspiciously.

'Yes, you have to leave the country.'

'Rudi what's wrong?' she asked yet again.

'Be patient,' he pleaded.

'I haven't got my passport,' she exclaimed.

'I have,' he patted his pocket and smiled. 'I've had it all night, just so that we wouldn't forget it.'

'Why must you be so mysterious?'

'Because it's a secret. You'll understand it all at the airport. There's no time to explain now.'

'I'm not going anywhere unless I do

understand,' she warned. 'The Prime Minister specifically said that there was an amnesty for the kidnappers and I don't see why I should run away.'

'Quite right,' Rudi agreed, 'but we don't want to take any chances, do we?'

She bit her lip with vexation. Here she was, with a hurriedly packed suit-case, no hat or gloves, being whisked off to the airport to be sent . . . where?

'Where am I going?'

'The airport.'

'I don't mean that. Where am I going to *from* the airport?'

'Frankfurt. It's the only flight there is.'

Of course, she thought, the only flight. She sat back, a little angry, and waited. It was not far now. Rudi parked the car just by the main entrance and she followed him inside. He took her along a corridor, knocked on a door and opened it. It was a small office, empty as an airline official had assured him it would be.

'Wait here a second, Liz. I shan't be long.'

He put down the case, winked and went out. She pulled a chair out from the desk and sat on it. Here she was determined to stay till she knew a lot more. The seconds went by and she began to tap her foot. What was keeping Rudi now?

The door opened and she glanced up, ready with questions. Her eyes widened.

'Hullo darling,' Charles Gresham said. 'You're late.'

'Charles!' She jumped to her feet and a moment later his arms were round her.

'What's happening?' she asked.

'We're flying to Frankfurt, then on to London. Everything is arranged. There will be a car to meet us at London airport.'

'Why?'

For answer he kissed her. She stood stock still for a few seconds, then began to respond to his kisses, and finally pushed him away frantically.

'What are you doing?' She was

blushing beautifully.

'I thought it was obvious. I'm kissing you. I intend to do a great deal of it in the weeks ahead, so I hope you can hold your breath for long periods.'

'What is all this about?' She looked charmingly bewildered.

He held her to him and smiled down at her.

'We're going to England to announce our engagement. We'll be married within the month. You, Elisabeth Renner, are going to marry me, that's what.'

'I never said any such thing.'

'Don't argue. I know all. Poor Kurt Schwarz.'

'What do you know about Kurt Schwarz?'

'It's a long story and I'll tell you all about it on the way to London. Meantime the flight has just been called and we'd better go and check in. First a kiss.'

'But . . . '

'Don't you love me, Elisabeth? Won't

you marry me? Please?'

'I do love you.' She said it quickly, without thinking, and then began to colour again.

'I thought you did. Rudi said so.'

'That Rudi . . . '

'Wonderful chap. Best brother-in-law a man ever had.'

'Oh Charles.' She surrendered. They could sort out all the loose ends later. This was what mattered. Her arms went round his neck and her mouth found his.

Rudi, opening the door, found them locked together. He grinned and coughed. He coughed again.

'I hate to do this,' he said very loudly, 'but it's time to go.'

They turned and smiled at him radiantly. Arm in arm the three of them walked along the corridor to Departure.

We do hope that you have enjoyed reading this large print book.

Did you know that all of our titles are available for purchase?

We publish a wide range of high quality large print books including:
Romances, Mysteries, Classics
General Fiction
Non Fiction and Westerns

Special interest titles available in large print are:
The Little Oxford Dictionary
Music Book, Song Book
Hymn Book, Service Book

Also available from us courtesy of Oxford University Press:
Young Readers' Dictionary
(large print edition)
Young Readers' Thesaurus
(large print edition)

For further information or a free brochure, please contact us at:
Ulverscroft Large Print Books Ltd.,
The Green, Bradgate Road, Anstey,
Leicester, LE7 7FU, England.
Tel: (00 44) **0116 236 4325**
Fax: (00 44) **0116 234 0205**

Other titles in the
Linford Romance Library:

DEAR OBSESSION

I. M. Fresson

Dr. Manley's wife Kate has allowed her son Johnnie to become an obsession, excluding the rest of her family. However, when the doctor takes a new partner, Dr. Paul Quest, everything changes. Johnnie becomes more independent and her husband less willing to go along with her obsession. Kate, now realising that she is in danger of losing her husband, must also accept the bitter truth: that Johnnie is capable of doing without her . . .

ALL TO LOSE

Joyce Johnson

Katie Loveday decides to abandon college to realise her dream of transforming the family home into a country house hotel and spa. With the financial backing of her beloved grandfather the business looks to be a runaway success. But after a tragic accident and the ensuing family squabbles Katie fears she may have to sell her hotel. When she also believes the man she has fallen in love with has designs on her business, the future looks bleak indeed . . .

ERRAND OF LOVE

A. C. Watkins

Jancy Talliman flies halfway around the world to Bungalan, in Australia, to renew an interrupted love affair with Michael Rickwood, who she'd met in London. She remains undaunted on discovering that he's unofficially engaged to Cynthia Meddow, especially given the support of Michael's brother Quentin, and his sister Susan. Jancy settles in a small town nearby. Then as she becomes involved with the townspeople, dam worker Arnulf, and Quentin, Jancy alters the very reason for her long journey south . . .

A NEW BEGINNING

Toni Anders

Rowena had only met her god-mother once, so why had Leonora Lawton left Cherry Cottage to her in her will? Should Rowena sell her bequest and continue to run her successful children's nursery, or make a new beginning in the chocolate box cottage two hundred miles away? The antagonism of Kavan Reagan, her attractive neighbour, who had hoped to inherit the cottage himself, only strengthens her resolve to make a new life for herself.

DAYS LIKE THESE

Miranda Barnes

Meg is devastated when her husband, the unreliable Jamie, leaves her. But life goes on. She develops a friendship with a colleague, Robert. Then Meg makes the bittersweet discovery that she is pregnant with Jamie's child. When Jamie reappears, she can't bring herself to tell him he is to be a father — until it's too late . . . Baby James arrives, and Meg resolves to be as good a parent as she possibly can. But it's Robert, not Jamie, she misses . . .

LOVE AT FIRST SIGHT

Chrissie L...

How could anyone not fall in love with Cameron? Handsome, rich, funny, caring — the sort of man every girl dreams of. And he had fallen in love with Megan. She couldn't say 'no' to his offer of marriage and she was swept along in a whirl of preparations. Was he just too good to be true? How well did she really know him? What was the old saying — 'marry in haste, repent at leisure'? She just hoped the second part wasn't true . . .